# A CAROL for MRS. DICKENS

## Also by
## REBECCA CONNOLLY

*A Brilliant Night of Stars and Ice*
*Under the Cover of Mercy*
*Hidden Yellow Stars*
*The Crime Brûlée Bake Off: A Claire Walker Mystery*

# REBECCA CONNOLLY

SHADOW
MOUNTAIN
PUBLISHING

Interior images: p. iii: Alexandr Sidorov/Adobe Stock; p. vi: JonnyJim/Getty Images; p. 10: Yuliya Kachan/Getty Images; p. 22: Grafissimo/Getty Images; p. 40: by artist Robert Barnes, duncan1890/Getty Images; p. 47: lynea/Adobe Stock; p. 60: little _airplane/Getty Images; p. 73: Yuliya Kachan/Getty Images; p. 78: whitemay/Getty Images; p. 86: Nastasic/Getty Images; p. 98: by artist Robert Barnes and engraver Joseph Swain, Cannasue/Getty Images; p. 113: tanys04/Getty Images; p. 122: duncan1890/Getty Images; p. 138: by artist Gustave Doré/public domain; p. 156: NSA Digital Archive/Getty Images; background: Maria/Adobe Stock.

Endsheets: Lisla/Shutterstock.com

© 2025 Rebecca Connolly

All rights reserved. No part of this book may be reproduced in any form or by any means without permission in writing from the publisher, Shadow Mountain Publishing®, at permissions@shadowmountain.com. The views expressed herein are the responsibility of the author and do not necessarily represent the position of Shadow Mountain Publishing.

This is a work of fiction. Characters and events in this book are products of the author's imagination or are represented fictitiously.

Visit us at shadowmountain.com

---

Library of Congress Cataloging-in-Publication Data

Names: Connolly, Rebecca, author.

Title: A carol for Mrs. Dickens / Rebecca Connolly.

Description: Salt Lake City : Shadow Mountain Publishing, 2025. | Summary: "Catherine Dickens, wife of Charles Dickens, experiences her own Christmas Eve transformation as she magically travels through her cherished memories to rediscover her lost love of Christmas"—Provided by publisher.

Identifiers: LCCN 2024058697 (print) | LCCN 2024058698 (ebook) | ISBN 9781639934294 (hardback) | ISBN 9781649334374 (ebook)

Subjects: LCSH: Dickens, Catherine, 1815–1879—Fiction. | LCGFT: Christmas fiction.

Classification: LCC PS3603.O54728 C37 2025 (print) | LCC PS3603.O54728 (ebook) | DDC 813/.6—dc23/eng/20250210

LC record available at https://lccn.loc.gov/2024058697

LC ebook record available at https://lccn.loc.gov/2024058698

---

Printed in Canada

PubLitho

10   9   8   7   6   5   4   3   2   1

＊

*To Catherine Hogarth Dickens.
I hope I did you justice and that
you accept this Christmas gift from me.
You are one of the noble women of history, and I salute you.*

*And to Areo chocolate melts for making
this write so merry and bright.*

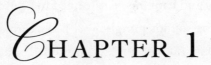

# Chapter 1

*London, England*
*December 24, 1851*

he holly and the ivy when they are both full grown..."

The carolers were out in full force, gathered in a small but boisterous semicircle outside the bookshop. Their voices were pure and their pitch fairly perfect, harmonizing in loveliness itself. The basket in front of them was half filled with goods and coins that passersby had offered for the group's beautiful talents.

Bits of snow piled in corners of the buildings, cleared from the paths shoppers would walk, but what remained was hardly enough to burden anyone.

Garlands of green, either real or paper, hung within nearly every shop window on either side of the road. Handbells and hanging bells seemed to be everywhere, the tinkling sounds mingling with the carolers' voices in discordant but not unpleasant ways. The air smelled of cinnamon, pine, and hot wine, all paired with the almost sugary scent of winter.

Magical, one might have called it.

But not Catherine Dickens. Not this year.

Kate was finishing her last errands before their family Christmas party this evening, and anything else, no matter how lovely, was a distraction from that course.

Everything was prepared—apart from what could only be accomplished today, of course. She had planned such parties for several years now, and it had become habit. The decorations were done, the bills of fare approved, the musicians scheduled, the entertainment engaged, her gown arranged. Kate had become skilled at being hostess, which had led her to publish her book on the subject this year.

A CAROL FOR MRS. DICKENS

Or her character—Lady Mariah Clutterbuck—
had, at any rate.

But this year felt different. Harder. Less festive.

Less like Christmas at all.

Losing her sweet Dora in April, at only eight
months of age, had broken her. For months, she had
been inconsolable, and her husband, Charles Dickens—
yes, *that* Charles Dickens—had done his utmost to
console her amid his own grief. His heart must have
contained some form of elasticity that Kate's did not,
for he was as cheery, dedicated, and energetic as ever.

Christmas had become his boon companion since
the success of his *Christmas Carol* story.

The man who had invented Christmas, some had
called him.

It felt like the whole city had found a renewed love
of Christmas and its particular season of goodwill and
thanksgiving through her husband's literary acumen.
But with the rise in charitable acts had also come the
rise of commercialization. Cards and toys and wrap-
pings and foods people would never have paid for
during the year were suddenly necessities.

Kate sometimes wondered if she was the only one who remembered that Christmas was a celebration of the birth of Christ.

Why had Christmas been forced to become something grand and spectacular when it had originally been the most simple, profound, exquisitely unnoticed event in all history? Apart from shepherds, choirs of angels, and a few wise men from the East, there had been nothing else.

Yet here in London, everyone was scrambling madly to be the most festive with the most elaborate celebrations to show off to all.

The quieter Christmas celebrations had never been a problem for Kate in the past, but those seemed to be long gone.

"Hark! The herald angels sing . . ."

The child within her suddenly mounted a rolling nudge to a rib, and Kate winced, both at the discomfort and at the reminder that this new baby was growing more and more. Christmas would seem a hollow one this year without Dora here to celebrate. She

## A Carol for Mrs. Dickens

ought to be toddling around and looking at the world with wonder.

Instead, she was gone, and this little one was as active and eager as any of its siblings. She placed a consoling hand on the rounded protrusion of her abdomen. Her tenth child, months from birth and already bearing the headstrong nature of the rest.

No wonder she was so exhausted this Christmas.

Most years, Christmas was a bright spot. But this Christmas Eve held some strange, mystical brightness that made her head ache and her eyes squint, disturbing the pattern of her life in a way she did not care for at all.

But she was a Dickens, which meant she had to celebrate Christmas as much as, if not more than, her husband.

She managed a small smile for the usual pair of children on the corner: a boy in a cap and a jacket that was too large for him and a smaller girl beside him, her blonde curls barely hidden by the kerchief wrapped about her head. Her tiny, knitted sweater had holes in it, but she didn't seem to notice. They were selling sprigs of holly from a basket, and Kate was half tempted to offer them some money, though she had no need for extra sprigs of holly. The house was practically bursting with festive decor as it was. The children were cheery enough little cherubs, the cold not seeming to perturb them in the least.

What sort of Christmas would they be having for themselves? Certainly not the kind of lavish party Charles insisted on having, nor their several guests.

Swallowing a sudden wash of tears, Kate approached them. "How much for the holly?"

"Tuppence, miss," came the boy's eager reply.

Kate nodded and pulled a coin from her reticule, placing it in the boy's open palm. "Please, take sixpence, but I only need one sprig."

The little girl's eyes widened. "'Ee certain, miss?"

"I insist." Kate took the holly from the little girl, smiling softly. "Merry Christmas."

"Merry Christmas," the girl replied with her own smile, her eyes crinkling sweetly.

With a nod, Kate turned away and tucked the sprig into her basket. She had found everything she needed

A CAROL FOR MRS. DICKENS

and started the short distance home to Tavistock House. Heaven knew she and Charles had finalized the bill of fare weeks ago, and the kitchen had been bustling for days. At Charles's insistence, they had hired additional kitchen staff for the day, though they would return for the annual Twelfth Night party, which would include most of the same guests, but a different air of celebration.

The first party they were hosting at their new home at Tavistock House, and it had to be a Christmas party followed in quick succession by one for Twelfth Night.

Two weeks and two parties to host.

Kate took a deep, weary breath.

There was a strange sense of invisibility as she walked among the other bustling Londoners without being jostled or acknowledged. Of being just another face in the crowd, another woman on an errand, another person shopping for last-minute items for a Christmas celebration, and nothing more.

She loved and hated this feeling. To be truly invisible for a time would have been a reprieve, but only if the burdens she carried would have also vanished.

Her home appeared before her, and Kate took several slow, deep breaths, willing the strength she required to distill upon her somehow. Within those walls, she had to be Mrs. Dickens, supportive wife and delighted hostess, for the rest of the day.

Kate entered the house, forcing her expression into one of serenity and composure. She had to become an actress now, and one of the best there was. Charles was far too observant, and if he had any indication that she was anything less than delighted about this evening's activities, she would hear about it.

All Kate had to do was make certain the house and food were ready for the party, though more than half of that responsibility would also be seen to by Charles purely out of his own excitement and desire to impress.

After fifteen years of marriage, she had learned how to cope and say nothing when he overstepped in such a way. Charles had always held concerns about and interest in the domestic details of the house, which was, ironically, how Kate had become such a well-practiced and seasoned hostess. His attention was not only a sign

## A Carol for Mrs. Dickens

of how deeply Charles cared about things but also of how focused he was on appearances.

His difficult past was partly to blame, but also his own exacting expectations of himself.

As his wife, Kate had to contend with those parts of him just as much as she did for the ones she loved most.

"Kate?" her husband called from the upstairs drawing room, where the entertaining would take place. "Did you get everything?"

Removing her hat, Kate restrained a sigh. "Yes, Charles. I shall be up in a moment."

"Hurry! I want you to see this!" His enthusiasm was blatant, and his sincerity not far behind.

Kate knew his tones well enough to know that he was as eager as any young boy about Christmas but also concerned that their guests would not find it as mesmerizing as he did.

She did not bother to remove her coat and started up the stairs with her basket. The house's decoration had all been put up at last: evergreen boughs and holly, hawthorn and rosemary, bay and hellebore, and even mistletoe hung from nearly every stretch of ceiling. The flat surfaces held much of the same, including so many candles that it would be a miracle if the house did not catch fire.

And she had not even seen the Christmas tree yet.

She smiled for Charles as she entered the room, his blessed Christmas tree perched on a table in the corner, some tapers and trinkets already strewn throughout the branches.

"It looks lovely, Charles," she told him as she approached.

He turned and gestured for her to give him the basket. "It needs more. Did you get everything?"

Kate tilted her head slightly as she handed over the basket. "You asked me that moments ago, and I said I did."

Charles shook his head and set the basket on the table beside the tree. "I wasn't listening. Ribbons! Excellent idea, Kate. These will look perfect among the branches and tapers."

## A Carol for Mrs. Dickens

"Those were actually . . ." Kate began, stepping forward before stopping and lamely concluding, "for the girls."

Charles was already draping the lengths of ribbon among bits of holly with bright-red berries, and if she tried to remove them now, there might not be a recovery.

Their daughters did not need new ribbons anyway. Not really.

"No pears?" Charles asked as he began to place the oranges, plums, and currants among the trinkets and toys, the watches and strings of beads, and the pieces of fruit that had been gold-leafed for a magical appearance.

Kate shook her head, though he would not see it. "There were no appealing ones. Only ripe pears with spots and such. It would have marred the appearance."

Charles nodded and continued his work. No opinions, only tasks.

"There are walnuts in the bottom there, if you would like them as well," Kate mentioned with a faint

*11*

gesture toward the basket. "It would seem you have everything else in hand."

"Would you check on how the food preparations are going, Kate?" Charles began arranging the new tapers among the existing ones. "With the additional hired staff below, I do not wish to take any chances."

It was no less than Kate had expected, and, quite honestly, a relief. If she was belowstairs with the kitchen staff, she would not have to face his erraticism nor his enthusiasm. She could conceivably remain down there until it was time to dress.

"Of course, Charles." She turned for the door, starting out of the room.

"Kate?"

She stopped and glanced back at him, making sure to smile. "Yes?"

His grin was wild and carefree, a memory of the young, energetic writer she had fallen in love with. "Thank you."

It ought to have been sweet. She could see the genuine light in him, but instead of feeling warmth, she felt cold by comparison.

A Carol for Mrs. Dickens

Still, his effort would not go unappreciated.

"Of course," Kate replied with a nod, allowing her smile to spread a bit farther. Then she left the room and made her way down to the kitchens.

Once she arrived, Kate stared around the large, whitewashed room in shock. There were far more people in the kitchens than she had ever had in such a space in her life, married or otherwise. But where it could have all been chaos and disorderliness, she found efficiency and structure, a smooth preparation for that evening's festivities.

An older woman in a linen cap that sported small green bows around its edges strode into the main kitchen, her matching dark-green dress mostly shielded by a slightly worn and freshly stained apron. Her face was round and her cheeks rosy, her mouth turned upward in a seemingly constant smile. A sprig of holly was pinned to her apron at her left shoulder, and the smaller one fixed to her cap was slightly askew.

Kate could not help but stare, noting that this woman looked almost startlingly like her aunt Christina. The same twinkle in her eye, the same softness to

13

her features, the same pucker of her upper lip. She was most certainly *not* her aunt, but the likeness immediately filled Kate with a sense of comfort and confidence.

And if the hint of flour on her hands and wooden spoon the woman waved about like a conductor's baton were any indication, she knew what she was about in the kitchens.

She saw Kate and smiled brightly, her cheeks creasing. "You mus' be Mrs. Dickens."

"I am," Kate replied on a heavy sigh. "I came down to go over the bill of fare one final time. Is Mrs. Rook about?"

"She's seein' to the turkey at the momen'," came the warm response. "Will you take a cuppa, madam? You look like you could use 'un."

A warm cup of freshly made tea in the kitchen sounded like perfection, and Kate nodded, allowing a tired smile to cross her lips. "That would be lovely, thank you." Her legs suddenly began to tremble and shake. Her knees buckling, Kate gripped the nearest chair quickly and sank onto it, forcing her breathing to slow and steady.

A CAROL FOR MRS. DICKENS

"Lord bless 'ee, madam!" The woman hurried over with a steaming cup of tea, a few Madeleine biscuits resting on the saucer. "Are 'ee well? Drink up. It is well-sugared."

Kate smiled as she took the tea. "Thank you. What is your name?"

"I am Mrs. Morley, madam," she replied with a quick bob before sitting on the chair beside her, looking Kate over with concern.

Sipping her tea, Kate nodded. "Thank you, Mrs. Morley. I am well, I think. Only tired."

Mrs. Morley tutted softly. "Life insists on going on when we would all prefer a rest, will it no'? And with 'ee expectin' another blessin' . . . 'Tis no wonder 'ee are tired."

Feeling her eyes begin to burn, Kate swallowed with some difficulty, willing back the tears. "I don't mind telling you, Mrs. Morley, that I wish we were not hosting this party tonight. You are right; I would prefer a rest. But my husband insists on quite the celebration. He does so love Christmas."

## Rebecca Connolly

Mrs. Morley cocked her head to one side. "And what about you, madam? Do you love Christmas?"

It was on the tip of Kate's tongue to retort immediately that she did, but she realized how hollow it would sound. She wanted to tell Mrs. Morley the truth, confide in her, which would be entirely inappropriate. Their difference in station, their working relationship, being practical strangers to each other . . .

But it did not feel that way. Indeed, Kate felt as though she might have actually been conversing with her aunt Christina or an old friend. Someone who cared and could offer her sympathy and advice. Someone she could trust.

Someone with whom she could connect.

And something about Mrs. Morley felt warm and merry, hopeful and bright. Perhaps it was only Christmas Eve, but this woman seemed to contain all the energy and magic of the holiday in her eyes and her smile. It was a balm to Kate's soul to even be near her, and it made her hope.

"I did once," Kate admitted as she looked down into her tea. "Not with the frenzy that Charles does,

## A Carol for Mrs. Dickens

and not in the same way, but I was deeply fond of the day itself."

"But not today."

Kate noticed the complete lack of question in Mrs. Morley's words and looked into the older woman's face, finding a striking amount of understanding in her fair eyes and gentle smile.

"No," Kate heard herself whisper. "And not for some time. I know the whole world has fallen in love with Christmas once more, and many ascribe that to Charles's book, which has certainly lifted his own feelings about the day to greater heights. I did not know greater heights were possible, but nevertheless . . ."

"You've not fallen in love with it in the same way," Mrs. Morley finished for her, nodding sagely and patting her arm. "The wives tend to be forgotten in such matters, I find. 'Tis no surprise to me that Mr. Dickens should be the same. In his enthusiasm, he forgets the work that any holiday or event is for the lady of the house. Who would be less than exhausted with all 'ee have to contend with, madam?"

"I miss the uneventful Christmases," Kate admitted, absently rubbing her aching bump. "This year feels like it is even more folderol than normal. Another theatrical for all of us to perform for the guests, another Christmas tree with exuberant decoration, another feast to stretch our finances—"

"And another bowl of punch Mr. Dickens will see to himself, as I understand it," Mrs. Morley added with a meaningful look.

Kate nodded in acknowledgment. "He will insist upon it, as he does every year. He is very good at it." Her gaze fell in exact time with her heart and landed on some small speck of floor beneath her feet. "How will I get through this night, Mrs. Morley? Or tomorrow, for that matter? Or New Year's? Or Twelfth Night?"

Mrs. Morley took her hand and squeezed it, her grip surprisingly strong and her hands perfectly warm. "Take heart, madam. Open your heart, if not your mind, and try to see the warmth Christmas once held for you, the fondness you once felt. Perhaps you might recapture a glimpse of those memories to bolster

A CAROL FOR MRS. DICKENS

you and find the balm you seek. Miracles take place at Christmas, and magic too. If you let Christmas in, madam, you may find it is already there."

It was sound advice, and Kate would not deny that she yearned for the happiness that Christmas had once brought her. To feel that there was a light in her eyes for others to see, just as she saw the light in her husband's eyes. To look forward with anticipation rather than dread of the festivities of the next two weeks.

And if, by some miracle, she managed to find that love and warmth again, perhaps it might also provide her with renewed strength and energy for the days and weeks ahead.

It felt like a daunting task, but something in this woman's plea reached deep within Kate's soul and lit a tiny wick of hope. And that was enough to make her brave.

"I will try, Mrs. Morley," Kate murmured with a nod. "I cannot promise success, but I will try."

Mrs. Morley gave her a fond, almost proud smile. "That's the ticket, madam. I will leave you to your tea now. Mrs. Rook has left me a mighty great list of tasks, and those marmalade tartlets are not going to fix themselves." She gave Kate an encouraging wink and rose, moving into another portion of the kitchen.

Kate quietly continued to sip her tea, waiting for Mrs. Rook to appear so they could confer on the progress of the bill of fare for the evening. Soon, Charles would come down to prepare his punch, and if Kate was just sitting there having tea . . .

Her husband's ability to become distracted by details was legendary in their home, and tonight was no time to revisit it.

Mrs. Rook came into the main portion of the kitchen, wiping her hands on her apron. "I am so sorry, madam. I had to be sure the turkey was seasoned appropriately while it roasts. Sometimes the hired help does not understand the particular requests of the hosting house, and it takes a little firmer hand to accomplish things." She sighed heavily, shaking her head. "You wish to confirm the bill of fare for the evening?"

Kate nodded, sipping the last of her tea before setting the cup aside. "Indeed, Mrs. Rook, as well as the timing of it all."

A CAROL FOR MRS. DICKENS

"Aye, Mrs. Dickens, let's get to it." Mrs. Rook pulled out her list and scratched at her slightly perspiring brow. "The vegetable and oxtail soup will be served first. Then we have turbot with smelts as well as shrimp sauce. For the main course, we have turkey, goose, tongue, and roast beef. Oyster curry, rice, pork cutlets, spinach, mashed and brown potatoes, and beetroot salad. For the third course, there is the cabinet pudding, marmalade tartlets, custards, macaroni, Charlotte Russe, and, of course, the plum pudding."

"That all sounds perfect," Kate said approvingly. "And the wines?"

"Topping has them all prepared and ready to serve as soon as requested."

Kate exhaled slowly, a contented peace settling over her. "Then we are ready, are we not?"

Mrs. Rook nodded, smiling in spite of her perspiration and preparations. "Indeed, we are, Mrs. Dickens."

# CHAPTER 2

Aha! There you have it. Sixteen guests and I've managed a fair cut of goose for every single one while still allowing for a leg for me!" Charles raised his carving tools triumphantly, laughing with the sort of victorious tone one might have expected on a jousting field.

The guests all laughed in appreciation and applauded him enthusiastically.

Kate smiled at her husband's childlike antics, which were all perfectly usual for his hosting persona. She was seated at the far end of the table from him, her task of serving the soup long over and now only engaged in passing the dishes around the table with the rest of the guests. Charles had carved up the fish for an earlier course and now took great delight in carving anything else that could be carved. He loved taking on this character of sorts, and his commentary on the dishes on the evening's bill of fare was always done with the varied voices that illuminated the number of literary characters who constantly lived in his mind.

"Mrs. Douglas," Charles said in a crisp, chirping voice as he sat, "you simply must give me your opinion on the beetroot salad. I never eat beetroot salad myself; I find the color excessively off-putting unless it is Christmas. But—oh my! It *is* Christmas! Do please pass me the festive salad, then! I shall eat with merriment, indeed, tonight!"

Mrs. Douglas laughed as she served herself salad and then handed the bowl to him. "Just as you please, Mr. Dickens."

But his attention had already been diverted. "Curry sauce! My good sir, do be generous with the delectable dressing." His voice was now that of an old, formal man constantly out of breath. "A good coating will enhance the pleasure of such a fine condiment."

And on it went, Charles spending as much time commenting comedically on each aspect of the meal as he did eating it. Truly, Kate was astonished that any of their guests managed to consume their food between the endless laughter and jests.

But this was Charles, who delighted in both food and in hosting. Kate might have been the one who published a book about the topic, but Charles had been the one to go through each bill of fare and recipe with his keen and appraising eyes, noting even something as small as the omission of salt from a pudding recipe. He was well-informed in the domestic art of cooking and took that aspect of hosting as seriously as he did the entertainment.

It was all a theatrical performance, the technical aspects of stage management and costuming just as crucial to the play's success as any of the actors or speeches given.

Full of vision was Charles Dickens, and those visions were expansive in their scope.

In a way, Kate counted it a blessing that he was so devoted to the entertainment at supper. It saved her the trouble of needing to be especially talkative, which allowed her to appear indulgent of her husband even if she simply did not wish to speak.

The conversation around the table was friendly and active, and there was something relaxing about the slight clinking of cutlery against china dishes in chorus around the room. If she focused on those sounds, the low hum of voices acting as a river beneath the ripples of clinks, Kate could almost feel herself at any other house party or dinner they'd ever hosted. An out of mind, out-of-body experience that did not require anything exceptional from her. Purely habitual and filled with rote memorization of tasks and responsibilities as well as points of conversation.

It was so simple a role to play, such a simple routine to slip into.

But no, it was Christmas, and thus all was destined to be different. Not just different but more. So much more.

Charles met her eyes and nodded once, which was

A CAROL FOR MRS. DICKENS

the signal for her to have the puddings brought in. She looked over at Topping, who served as the messenger, and gave him the same sign of a single nod. He returned the gesture and stepped out for a moment. Their additional staff stepped forward to remove the guests' empty plates, filing out of the dining room in a neat, silent line.

With perfect timing, Topping reentered the dining room with the flaming Christmas pudding, the platter lined with sprigs of deep-green holly, their bright-red berries brilliantly standing out against the rich brown pudding. Behind Topping were additional kitchen staff bringing in the rest of the desserts for the guests.

The cabinet pudding, Charlotte Russe, custards, macaroni, and tartlets all paled in comparison to the plum pudding, which was how it was designed to be, but each dessert looked remarkable and beautiful in its own right. Kate accepted the applause from the guests at this display as a victory for herself, but she did not make any moves to acknowledge it as such. Just something to treasure up in her heart and look back on with pride.

27

A glimmer of promised Christmas magic.

Charles made some sort of declaration of festive platitudes over the pudding and the like, praising the ingenuity in the creation and pomp of such things with unnecessary zeal. One need never question his love for foodstuffs, that was for certain.

The plum pudding was sliced and served up for each guest while they added other sweet selections to their plates, the hums and smiles of satisfaction and delight evidence enough of their pleasure.

That was just as Kate had hoped. If all were well-fed and well-satisfied, the rest of the evening was destined to be equally agreeable and successful.

Just the sort of sated, festive mood that Charles would wish for.

"A toast, ladies and gentlemen!" Charles suddenly announced, startling Kate out of her reverie. He was standing at the head of the table, his wine glass aloft.

The gentlemen rose with their glasses, looking at him in expectation. The ladies held theirs in anticipation as well. Kate gave her husband a curious look, but he only smiled.

A CAROL FOR MRS. DICKENS

"To the hostess of our evening, whose careful, considerate  festive planning made our delicious feast just as it ought to be." He indicated Kate with his glass, his smile broadening. "My wife, Mrs. Catherine Dickens."

"Mrs. Dickens," the guests intoned in unison, each one taking a sip.

"And to the most entertaining, festive, amiable host, the soul of Christmas himself, Charles Dickens!" Mr. Cready called, toasting toward Charles.

Kate tried not to laugh in faint irony, especially when the rest of the group gleefully took up this second toast. Had she not been thinking earlier in the day how people exaggerated her husband's influence on Christmas and its season? How they missed the meaning and reason for it in lieu of the more flagrant embodiments of celebration rather than the truer heart?

Yes, her husband was all fervor and glee, especially where Christmas was concerned, and yes, he was particularly amiable and entertaining as a host, but did the overly flattering toast have to come so promptly on the heels of his sweet tribute toward her?

Was that such a selfish, horrible thought to have?

*29*

If Charles noticed, he gave no indication. He gestured for them all to sit, encouraging them to finish their puddings, and it was only a few moments more before the plates were emptied.

Leading the guests away from the table, Charles nearly skipped his way upstairs, leaving no question as to his feelings for the night and its continued festivities.

Kate was more sedate in her motions, waiting for the last of the guests to depart the room before following.

One of the more rotund guests slowed his step to speak with her as they moved.

"Ah, the turkey was the finest to be seen, Mrs. Dickens. And so perfectly stuffed and flavored! And the artistry with which it was carved and plated up for us . . . My, it was simply the finest feast I have ever known, even at Christmas! So very kind of you to also provide goose for the feast, and a very, very fine goose it was. Such generosity of food and drink, it is enough to make any soul quite merry, is it not?"

Kate smiled with all the benevolence of a gracious

A CAROL FOR MRS. DICKENS

hostess. "Thank you, Mr. MacNeil. Charles does love to carve himself, and he does such a fine job of it, does he not? Be sure to have some of his Christmas punch, if you have not already. It is truly worthy of the holiday."

Mr. MacNeil, who had indulged quite steadily in the various wines and liqueurs during the meal, chortled in anticipation and hastened his steps to follow the others.

"Shall we have some dancing now, friends?" Charles cried as he waved everyone toward the schoolroom they had turned into a ballroom.

There were resounding cries of approval from the guests, all caught up in the spirit and excitement of the moment and of Charles's clear enthusiasm. Kate moved into the schoolroom and nodded to the hired musicians who were comfortably chatting among themselves, indicating for them to begin playing. They quickly assembled themselves into their preferred grouping, music beginning to fill the space.

Charles led Mrs. Montrose into the room rather grandly, though the older woman would almost certainly not be dancing that evening due to a weakness in her right knee. She took one of the first available chairs in the space and watched with delight as others began to line up to dance.

To no one's surprise, Charles was among the first group of dancers, and the musicians began a polonaise. Charles was nothing if not a stickler on the proper order of things, and this joyous figure and dance formation was one he always insisted on opening with. Those watching soon began to clap in time with the music, and the dancers stepped lively across the floor.

A waltz came next, and Charles made the rounds of the room to mingle with those not dancing. Kate watched him do so, marveling at the ease with which he could fall into conversation with anyone on nearly any topic and how laughter was almost certain to follow.

She had been doing the same, of course—speaking with as many guests as she could as well as appreciating the dancing—but Charles had a natural way and air about him that made him the most congenial of men. And when he was also hosting an event, those qualities seemed to become more enhanced.

## A Carol for Mrs. Dickens

No one commanded attention in a room like Charles, especially at Christmas.

Kate did not necessarily wish to command attention, and she had grown perfectly accustomed to being Mrs. Dickens rather than Kate Dickens, but neither did she wish to be overlooked.

Charles Dickens *was* Christmas. Mrs. Dickens was . . . his wife.

Kate's smile felt thin as she walked among her seated guests, offering glasses of Charles's punch or slices of pudding, plates of madeleines and gingerbread biscuits, anything to make the guests feel welcome and festive. Her face began to ache with her forced joviality, the music now grating discordantly in her ears. How could such delightful sounds, particularly mingled with laughter, become so irritating in a single moment?

She glanced at the dancing, noting the ebullient expressions on every dancer's face. It was as though dancing was the gateway to such joy, and yet similar emotions were on display for those watching as well. She could not dance in her condition, but she could do as Mrs. Morley had suggested. She could try to open her heart, seek for joy, and let the warmth in.

Charles rejoined the dancing on the next song, insisting on a polka, which their daughters had taught him the year before. The laughter rose to an even greater pitch, leaving Kate behind.

She did not wish to be left behind.

*Open your heart.*

Kate listened to the music with greater intensity, focusing almost entirely on her heart and willing it to open. She imagined great dark curtains being pulled back, revealing a window glistening with winter frost. Light was peeking through, but could she open it? Could she find a way to have more?

The polka finished to much applause, Charles applauding most of all. He gestured quickly for the musicians to play something else, all the while moving out of the dancing space. He shook hands with some of the observing gentlemen, laughing breathlessly and making a show of his fatigue for everyone watching.

Kate wasn't entirely certain what her husband intended to do next, but there was a soft sense of fondness

## A Carol for Mrs. Dickens

at this illustration of his nature. His theatrical, amusing, personable nature captivated audiences when he was on stage, either in character or in speech. What a character Charles Dickens was. How much of that had she seen in him early on?

To her surprise, Charles made his way over to her, putting a hand on her arm even as he looked back at the dancing. "Going well, is it?" he asked her, his hair in almost complete disarray.

"It seems to be," Kate replied, taking a moment to fuss his hair back into some sense of order.

When she was done, he took her hand and kissed it, his eyes filled with a sweetness she adored. His color was as high as his energy, bright-red patches dotting his cheekbones as though painted by hand. She could feel his pulse through the palm on her arm. "You are enjoying yourself," she murmured with a smile she could not help.

"I am, I won't deny it," Charles quipped as he gave her a wide grin. "Several compliments on the punch this year, of course, and I anticipate the party will only grow more jovial as the night goes on."

Kate's smile took on a wry turn. "It always does with your punch, Charles."

He playfully considered that. "Yes, well, not everyone has my restraint for the drink, my dear Kate. I appreciate the thing, but that does not mean I must always imbibe."

"Yes, I know." She sighed. "Would you like to have some singing later as well? Mrs. Black could play, if the musicians need a respite."

"Oh, we must have singing!" Charles insisted. He looked back at the dancing, nearly bouncing on his heels as though he longed to rejoin them. "It would not be a Christmas party if we did not sing! Perhaps later, as you suggest." His hand fell from her arm, and he reached over to pluck a gingerbread biscuit from the plate. "After a few more dances, I can invite our guests to the Christmas tree to select a gift."

"That sounds lovely," Kate admitted as she nodded. "And perhaps—" She cut herself off as Charles walked away, moving directly to one of the guests and immediately engaging the fellow in conversation, half-eaten biscuit in hand and all.

A CAROL FOR MRS. DICKENS

There was really nothing to do but sigh once more. Charles was as easily distracted as he was imaginative, and she had long ago learned not to take offense at it.

But it did not follow that it was not still frustrating.

With a slight grinding of her teeth, Kate shook her head. Perhaps if she could also dance the night away, she would feel differently. She put a hand to her abdomen without thinking, her attention drawn toward thoughts of her children. They'd had their own version of the Christmas feast in the nursery, and soon enough, her older children would be dancing with the guests at these parties.

Charley was already fourteen, and it would be difficult to treat him as a child for much longer. Mamie and Katey were on the cusp of young womanhood at thirteen and twelve, respectively, and as for the rest . . .

Childhood passed so very swiftly, the moments of sweetness so often lost in day-to-day life.

With a surge of longing, Kate started up the flight of stairs toward the bedrooms. As she had expected, the nursery was dark, and her little ones were sleeping.

Francis would soon go off to school and no longer remain in this room with his siblings, but for now, he was content enough to be with his brothers. Alfred wanted to do whatever Francis was doing, so his adjustment to the change would be the most striking. Sydney and Harry were still so young that they could rightfully be considered cherubs in both appearance and nature, having lost none of the plumpness in their baby cheeks.

How she loved these sweet boys! The empty crib to one side of the room was a poignant reminder to her of what had been lost as well as what was soon to come, and both held special places in her heart. And what about her oldest babies quietly spending the evening in their bedrooms? The ones who would soon barely need a mother at all?

How could she make Christmas lovely for any of them when it felt so empty for herself?

Did they not deserve more?

In that moment, a bright, white light illuminated the room, centering everywhere and nowhere at once. Kate immediately started toward the children, worried the light would waken and frighten them. But they did not stir nor rouse even in the slightest.

Kate looked around, confused as the light grew brighter and brighter, forcing her to squint even as she tried to shield her eyes from the ever-increasing whiteness around her. Even closing her eyes, the white seemed to seep through the cracks, filling her vision, her hair, her limbs, her breath—everything was suddenly white and warm and tingling.

A rush of wind filled her ears, and she had the sensation that she was flying or falling, a swift movement without her arms or legs contributing anything at all.

And then there was solid ground beneath her feet again. The rushing faded from her ears, and the blinding whiteness dimmed rapidly into nothingness.

Heart racing, Kate slowly opened her eyes, blinking as she looked around.

Where was she?

# CHAPTER 3

t took her a few moments to account for what she was seeing, and then some additional moments for any of it to make sense.

The space before her was the nursery from their previous home at Devonshire Terrace, but there were only four beds, some of them quite small. There were fewer games and toys strewn about than she was used to, and the sun streamed through the windows with the perfect bliss often depicted in paintings.

"Make haste, Mama! Papa is taking us to a toy shop! He says we shall get presents there!"

Kate turned at the young, eager cry echoing in the halls. She knew the voice well but had not heard it in

41

several years. The high-pitched tones belonged to her son Charley, so many years younger than his present age.

How could she be hearing it now?

Kate hurried out of the nursery, wondering if she might be given a glimpse of her sweet boy as he had once been.

"All right, Charley," she heard her own voice reply brightly. "I am coming."

Kate stumbled a step. It had been her voice, certainly enough, but not one of those words had come from her lips.

Not at this moment.

The voices were coming from below her, so she quickened her pace down the stairs, doing her best to stay as quiet as possible. But she had to know—had to see—if what she was hearing could possibly be real.

Or was she, perhaps, succumbing to some new and disastrous trouble with her nerves?

She did not falter on the familiar stairs of Devonshire Terrace, and she was soon able to peer down into the entryway of the house, holding her breath.

A CAROL FOR MRS. DICKENS

And oh! There in their winter outerwear stood her four eldest children, all tiny creatures as they had once been, and Kate herself stood among them, wrapped in a green plaid mantle and smiling around at her eager young ones, each practically dancing with excitement.

"Now, children," Kate watched and heard the younger version of herself say, "Papa will be taking us to a toy store in Holborn, which is such a distance that we are going to take a coach. He is fetching one for us now. You must all be on your very best behavior and thank the coachman for taking us. Do you understand?"

All four heads bobbed repeatedly.

Younger Kate smiled at them and smoothed young Walter's plump cheek.

By the look of him, he must have been barely two years of age, and he would never have understood what she was asking of him, but he would follow the example of his older siblings, as always.

*This must be a memory*, Kate thought. The interactions felt so familiar, and yet she could not recall any of these specifics.

"And do be considerate," younger Kate told the children, "when Papa allows you to choose a toy. We must be able to bring the toy back home with us, after all, so you mustn't select anything that will not fit in the coach, must you?"

The children giggled and shook their heads, though Katey frowned a little as she did so.

She was their little temper pot of a child. "Lucifer Box," her father had called her then, a name said with as much affection as truth.

No one would ever dissuade the determined Katey from what she felt was her due, and Kate hoped that the girl would never lose that spirit.

The door to the house opened, and Charles appeared, gesturing out into the streets. "Presenting," he announced with grand rolling of his *R*'s, "the finest transportation accommodation seen since the Lord Mayor of London purchased his new barouche summer before last! Do, please, come and take your seats, at your leisure." He offered his hand to Mamie as though she were a duchess, leading her out of the house.

Kate descended the rest of the stairs, wondering

A CAROL FOR MRS. DICKENS

how she could possibly join them in the carriage for this venture. She did not want to miss a single moment, and while she recollected that she and Charles had, indeed, taken the children to select toys in Holborn, she could not remember any details. Too much had happened, and too much took up her thoughts.

She watched as her younger self took Walter's hand to lead him out after Charley and Katey. Watched as Charles swung each child into the coach with his infectious playfulness. Watched as the two of them shared a fond smile for each other as Charles then helped his Kate into the coach as well.

He followed her in, the door was shut, and the carriage rolled away from Devonshire Terrace.

With a single blink, Kate suddenly found herself in a beautiful toy store wreathed in red and gold bunting while the shelves were filled with china dolls, carousels, regiments of toy soldiers, animal figures beyond imagination, puppets and puppet shows, stuffed and cuddly dogs, rabbits, and bears, and more. As far as the eye could see, there were toys. The floor boasted rows of rocking horses along with barrels of stick horses, crates of toy swords and shields, and several impressive-looking cricket bats.

The bell at the front of the store rang, and out of pure instinct, Kate turned toward it. Her eyes fell upon her children as they entered, Charles and her younger self close behind. She watched as each of the children glanced around the store, eyes widening the more they saw.

"Well," Charles said with a laugh, putting his hands on the backs of Charley and Katey, "what are you waiting for? Find the toy you've always dreamed of! No restrictions! Find your Christmas present! Go, little strangers, go!"

The children darted off with peals of laughter and glee while Charles chortled with delight. Mamie and Katey swept right past Kate, but her skirt remained unmoved in their wake.

Could they not see her, then? Any child would surely have taken greater pains to avoid a stranger in their path, even with such a single-minded focus on prospective toys.

Was she here or was she not here?

## A Carol for Mrs. Dickens

"Charles, think of the cost!" the younger Kate scolded half-heartedly, looking concerned as well as amused. "And what if Walter wants one of those immense rocking horses? We cannot take that in the coach with us."

Charles grinned at her, looking so like their children at that moment. He put a hand on her arm. "Kate, it's Christmas Eve! And with the success of my little ghost story, we can afford to be a bit extravagant in our gifts for the children. If Walter wants a large rocking horse, we will have it delivered to our home. Christmas

should be the most wonderful time of the year for all of us, but especially for the children. Let us spoil them while we can, eh?" He patted her arm, winked, and moved away to follow the children.

How could Kate have forgotten this day and this experience? Surely it ought to have stood out in her mind through all these years.

"Oh, Mr. Dickens!" the shopkeeper's voice suddenly cried. "Your Christmas Carol was so remarkable a tale, so moving a read. I wept shamelessly by the end and have determined I must do better by my fellow man."

Kate glanced over at the exchange, Charles's low response lost on her as he shook the man's hand, smiling in encouragement.

Ah, this must be 1843, then. Just after *A Christmas Carol* had been published and was surprising all of London.

No wonder Charles was in such a giving, generous mood. Yes, Christmas always brought that out in him, but he was still fairly fiscally responsible where the children were concerned.

A Carol for Mrs. Dickens

This year, however, it seemed that was different.

Kate looked back at herself, still standing near the front of the store, unmoved, for all intents and purposes. She would be pregnant with Francis, and heavily so. As though her present thoughts were connected to her past self, she watched as her hand went to the distinctly rounded bulge in her abdomen, partially obstructed by the voluminous skirts and outerwear.

She would have Francis less than a month from this Christmas Eve, and her healing from that birth would be one of her better ones. Her spirits were higher, her physical recovery swifter, and her energy for life and motherhood more enhanced. It had been a beautiful time of life, which was something she seemed to have lost in the intervening years.

This younger, more hopeful version of herself, who had still experienced hardship and the loss of one pregnancy, still bore a vibrancy that Kate envied.

Envious of herself. How could that even be possible?

Her younger self suddenly looked directly at her, a knowing smile on her lips.

*49*

Kate looked behind her, certain there must be someone else nearby. But there was no one and nothing. She turned back, noting the bemused tilt to her own young mouth. Then, of all things, her younger self walked toward her.

So was she visible after all?

"It's all right," younger Kate said as she approached. "Only I can see you."

Kate swallowed, her throat tightening with a combination of fear, anticipation, and confusion. "I think I would remember an occasion where I spoke to my older self."

Young Kate chuckled easily. "Of course you would. But this is a memory, Kate. *Your* memory. It is not actively happening but already has. I am a memory of you as you were, as is this toy shop. As are the children. As is Charles."

Kate looked around again, trying to see everything with clear eyes. How could something in memory be this clear and this real? Ought it not be tinged with age and a trifle hazy in places? Should not bits and pieces

A CAROL FOR MRS. DICKENS

be unclear or constantly shifting as so often seemed to be the case when one attempted to recall specifics?

She reached out and touched the nearest box wrapped in brown paper and tied with strings to appear as a festive present. Yes, her fingers felt the texture of the paper and the solidness of the object beneath it. She could run her hand over its surface just as though she really were touching it.

So all of this was real . . . and yet it was not?

"Peculiar, isn't it?" Young Kate laughed again and sighed, putting her hands comfortably inside a pale muff. "I am glad you've chosen this memory. I am so happy here. The children are such fun ages, and they adore Charles so fervently. Last evening, he made up a story for them before bed, roaring and stomping to such a degree that they were far too full of giggles to sleep for ages. But I didn't mind. I wasn't angry with him, nor impatient with them. The sound of their laughter is the most beautiful music in the world."

Girlish giggles came from one section of the store, and a surge of warmth immediately flooded Kate's heart and made her smile. That would be Mamie and Katey,

*51*

either making each other laugh or their father doing so. It was the silliest, sweetest sound—those young angelic voices raised in amusement. Some parts of her heart ached at hearing it again after so long a time.

Her little boys must laugh as well. Surely she heard them from time to time, and was that not a sound to be adored? Had she forgotten to listen for it?

She blinked, and the scene changed once more, now placing her in the kitchens of Devonshire Terrace, her husband and children gathered with her. From the bowls of raisins and currants on the counter to the floured cloth on the surface beside them, Kate could tell they were mixing a Christmas pudding. But, as any seasoned cook knew, a proper Christmas pudding would have already been prepared by Christmas Eve to let the flavors sink in before boiling it shortly ahead of the Christmas feast.

This must have been the pudding for the children.

Kate watched as Mamie carefully added candied peel to the mixture, Charles sprinkling additional breadcrumbs in as she did so. Then Charles lifted Katey,

A Carol for Mrs. Dickens

allowing her to dump in her bowl of currants. Walter flung in raisins. Charley tipped in the allspice and salt.

Charles took over mixing the pudding as the young Kate added eggs and milk to the mixture, the children watching in fascination as the consistency changed and became a doughy texture. There were giggles and shared looks of amusement as Charles tipped the mixture onto the cloth with particularly entertaining sound effects, and then scattered applause as he tied the cloth with great flourish.

"Now, my students," he intoned in a crafted French accent, "we will boil the pudding until it is perfect. Hours, it will take. Hours and hours. And then . . ." He kissed the air loudly. "Perfection, *oui*? *Oui*. And we shall place upon it a tiny bit of . . . What is the word? Rosebush? A fern, perhaps?"

"Holly!" Charley and Mamie shouted together as Katey and Walter laughed themselves silly.

"Ah, *bien sûr*! How could I forget?" He slapped his forehead, then handed the pudding to Kate, who was shaking her head even as her shoulders shook with laughter.

53

She turned and placed the pudding in the boiling water over the fire before brushing her hands on her apron. Then she turned to the children, her smile bright. "There. Now it boils. So, shall we turn our attention to decorating the house for tonight?"

The children cheered and raced out of the kitchen, Charles hard on their heels and cheering with just as much exuberance.

Kate looked at her young self and watched the smile fade a little with fatigue. She heard the sigh and felt comfortable enough with the situation to approach.

"Is it too much?" she asked. "Don't you resent being left to clean this mess yourself?"

Young Kate looked at her in surprise. "No. The moment of solitude is a lovely respite. With Charles taking such an eager interest in the exact placement of each bough of holly and ivy, it is far better that he be with the children to do that while I see to the tasks down here. And the children will be so pleased to show me their work later, which allows me to praise them and shower them with affection. Soon, they'll be back with their nursemaid and the evening will be

A CAROL FOR MRS. DICKENS

without them. What would be gained by limiting their investment in our Christmas celebrations simply so the kitchen might be clean in a shorter amount of time?"

"But you miss things," Kate whispered, wishing she could be with Charles and the children to see their young faces so alight with the giddiness their father seemed born with.

Her younger self surveyed her with kind eyes, tilting her head slightly. "I don't believe I do. I simply experience different ones. The memory my children just made down here? They will always have that. The memory they are creating now with their father? They will always have that too. And besides, he will soon be distracted with his next characters and work. I must take advantage of his desire to be like a child with the children while I can, else they might not know the man he truly is. And I love the way they love him." She smiled further, her eyes seeming to grow moist, and she nudged her head toward the stairs.

Kate could not possibly join a gathering she had not witnessed, could she? There was no memory to visit where no memory was created. Could she also

55

visit her imagination? That would surely defy whatever logic and bounds she was restricted by now, were such things in place.

Still, she started for the stairs, and, on a blink, found herself up in the schoolroom. Based on the light streaming through the windows, it was later in the day, and she saw herself sitting in a chair while Charles played with the children.

He had a blindfold around his eyes, and his hands were stretched out before him, trying to catch any of the children. The children were not particularly skilled in their efforts to evade their father, though they could hardly be blamed for that. Charley was only six, after all, and Walter nearly three with the girls sandwiched between them in age. There was no stealth in those years, and that was part of the charm.

Still, Charles made a decent effort at pretending it was difficult to tell where they were. Catching them was seemingly impossible, and there were enough close calls to convince the children that they were succeeding in their deception.

## A Carol for Mrs. Dickens

Kate walked over to her younger self with confidence, knowing she would not be observed by anyone else. This time, she had nothing to ask and nothing to say. She only wanted the chance to observe the scene through her younger eyes, as much as possible.

If it was at all possible.

"I would be up there with them, you know," the younger Kate murmured. "Were it not for this interesting condition of mine. Though I suppose it is no longer interesting by this number." She smiled to herself and gently rubbed her stomach.

Kate put a hand on her own, less-pronounced bulge. "No, it is not."

"But it does so add to the love in my life," her younger self went on. "Each dear face, sweet laugh, caring heart, and mischievous personality makes my own heart grow, and somehow my ability to love grows with it. It takes nothing away; it only gives."

"And exhausts," Kate added before she could stop herself.

She felt the gaze of this younger version, this

younger memory, of herself, but did her best not to look at her.

"Life exhausts," came the kind, soft rebuke. "It is the nature of being alive. It is our mortal experience. Would you resent the love, laughter, and warmth in your life because it also comes with fatigue, loss, and irritation? We take the good with the bad, Kate. And there is always good."

The pounding that had begun in Kate's heart now became thunderous, each pulse ricocheting through her neck and palms with an unnerving potency. She could feel the truth in those words sink into her with each beat, but her mind still whirled.

There was too much now to truly believe and feel this, was there not?

Kate looked at her younger self, somehow seeing the understanding and wisdom in her own eyes despite this past version of herself only knowing half of what the present Kate had endured.

How was any of this possible? How could she advise herself in such a way?

How could a memory be so perfectly vibrant?

## A Carol for Mrs. Dickens

She closed her eyes, shaking her head a little.

And then a pulling sensation tugged at her shoulders and her waist, the shade of light behind her eyelids finding a new darkness she had never known.

# CHAPTER 4

When her eyes opened, Kate found herself back in the doorway of her children's nursery at Tavistock House, their sleeping figures still tucked neatly in their individual beds. She gripped the doorframe a moment, unaware of how much time had passed or if she had moved a single inch.

She blinked hard, wondering if she might be transported once more, but nothing happened.

Curious, indeed.

Kate swallowed, finding a surprising amount of moisture in her throat and eyes as she did so. Were those tears for what she had experienced or for being returned to her present? Her emotions were not well-defined, let alone easily explained.

Still, if she had returned to her present, there was a party taking place below, and she would have guests to see to.

She smiled toward her sleeping boys, then turned a fond gaze down the corridor toward the rooms where her older children would either be sleeping or quietly reading in bed. She moved back to the stairs and descended, finding that smile for her children easy enough to keep on her lips for any guests she might encounter.

"Oh, there 'ee are, Mrs. Dickens!"

Kate paused as Mrs. Morley approached on the stairs, cheeks still rosy red. "Is everything well, Mrs. Morley?"

"Oh, yes, madam," Mrs. Morley assured her with a smile, slightly out of breath. "I jus' wanted to return something to 'ee." She held out a sprig of holly.

Blinking, Kate frowned slightly at it. "Where did you get that?"

"It was on the kitchen floor, madam. 'Ee must have

## A CAROL FOR MRS. DICKENS

dropped it when 'ee took dizzy." She gently pressed it into Kate's hand. "I thought it might help 'ee find that love of Christmas tonight."

Kate felt a burst of warmth crackle within her chest and begin to glow, radiating the beauty and light she had felt so purely in her memory only moments before. "Perhaps it might," she murmured with a nod.

Mrs. Morley winked in encouragement and turned away, hurrying back down the stairs toward the kitchens.

It was odd, but Kate was almost certain she had placed the sprig of holly in the basket earlier, and she could not recollect ever removing it, let alone having it on her person when she went down to the kitchens. But she had not been paying particular attention, so perhaps she was mistaken.

She shook her head and tucked the sprig of holly into her brooch. She had promised to open her heart tonight, or try to, at least. And the holly sprig might help her achieve that, especially with the delights ahead.

Once the greenery was securely fixed, she started toward the party again. What excuse would she give

63

REBECCA CONNOLLY

if she had been gone awhile? There were a few reasons vague enough to be credible for a hostess and others more fitting for any mother to understand, but would any of them actually come from her mouth?

Thankfully, she heard knocking at the front door, which would be reason enough to be absent from the party for a moment. With hurried steps, she continued to the ground floor and to the door, opening it with a warm and ready smile.

"Merry Christmas!" a trio called out with broad grins.

Kate recognized them at once as their former neighbors from the residence in Devonshire Terrace: Mr. Banks, his wife, and his sister. She beamed at them all. "Dear friends! Thank you so much, and merry Christmas to you! Won't you come in and join us?"

Mr. Banks shook his head. "Thank you, but no, Mrs. Dickens. We are simply delivering compliments of the season and a collection of gifts for your family. A bit of goodwill never goes amiss, yes?" He gestured to his sister.

Miss Banks produced a basket adorned with a

## A Carol for Mrs. Dickens

bright-green ribbon and filled with bottles of wine, knitted goods, oranges, toy soldiers, and hair ribbons.

Kate's eyes filled with hot tears as she took the basket from them. "This is so lovely. Thank you most sincerely. Will you take something in return?"

"We will not," Mrs. Banks replied with a laugh, holding up her hands as though to press the offer away. "We are well aware how much you give, Mrs. Dickens, and we have more than enough. God bless you."

"And you," Kate managed hoarsely, nodding additional thanks.

The Banks family waved and trotted down the street, followed slowly by a wagon filled with more baskets in the back.

Gifts from generous souls without any expectation of a return. What a beautiful, poignant note to strike on this Christmas Eve!

Kate closed the door, swiping at the warm tears on her cheeks. She looked down at the basket, shaking her head. The thought behind it mattered more than what it contained, but she could see very clearly what the delighted responses of her children would be in the morning.

And the girls *would* have new ribbons after all.

*We take the good with the bad. And there is always good.*

Setting the basket in the parlor, Kate pinched her cheeks both to bring more color to them and to remove the traces of tears as she moved upstairs to rejoin Charles and the guests.

"To the Christmas tree!" she heard Charles call and smiled faintly in amusement. If he bellowed much louder, he would wake the children, and that would certainly not please the upstairs maid.

Most of the guests had followed Charles into the drawing room and were now mingling and admiring the Christmas tree or warming themselves by the great fire.

After a long moment to survey the scene and make notes of the positions of various guests, Kate began her rounds among them. It was a delicate art, finding the balance she needed for such conversations, and had become a very comfortable routine of sorts. She

## A Carol for Mrs. Dickens

took great care to vary her topics, asking after a guest's loved ones, wishing them the compliments of the season, ensuring they had gotten enough to eat, inquiring as to recent theater visits or concerts, discussing interesting travels, and anything else that might provide good conversation as opposed to the superficial sort. She had always prided herself on remembering particular details of guests and being able to converse rather specifically with them from one party or event to the next. Even if she became distracted by duties or interruptions as hostess, she always made a point to return to a guest and continue the discussion as much as she could.

She never wished for a single guest to believe themselves forgotten at one of her parties, and she firmly believed that dedicated attention was a certain way to show her gratitude for their acceptance of the invitation.

Charles might be the highlight of any gathering they hosted, but Kate had to be the most capable and memorable supporting act possible. Whenever people spoke of a party hosted by Charles Dickens, his wife would also be mentioned, and those mentions needed to be universally positive.

After her experience outside her children's nursery, Kate found her hostess routine somehow lighter now. Easier. More natural. Less forced. Her smiles came more readily, her tone had taken on a new brightness, and her interest in the conversations she had with guests was more sincere. The fatigue in her body, which she was fully aware of, was not such a burden, and there was no prickle of irritation at the edges of her thoughts and feelings.

What a refreshing alteration this was!

"Come closer, everyone," Charles suddenly called, gesturing for the guests to gather around the fire and Christmas tree. "Let us have some singing and story-telling, shall we? Or perhaps . . . a reading?" He waggled his eyebrows, and, as he'd surely intended, the group applauded eagerly.

Kate shook her head fondly. Charles loved to read from his beloved Christmas Carol on such an occasion, both to engage in the dramatics and to remind others of the meaning behind his work. Of course, it was not

## A Carol for Mrs. Dickens

often that their guests focused on the meaning more than the performance, but Kate always hoped that they would return home with higher thoughts than the fleeting and simple enjoyment of his recitation.

Charles pulled a well-worn copy of his book from the mantel, where he had undoubtedly set it for just such a purpose.

He turned a few pages, then smiled to himself and cleared his throat. "Perhaps I shall start from the delightful Ghost of Christmas Present? Ahem. 'The moment Scrooge's hand was on the lock, a strange voice called him by his name, and bade him enter. He obeyed. It was his own room. There was no doubt about that,'" Charles read in his usual, if slightly more formal voice. "'But it had undergone a surprising transformation.'"

Kate knew this portion of the story well, as it was one of Charles's favorite passages to read when their children were not present to act out the scenes. This was the elaborate description of all the glorious decorations and foodstuffs that filled Scrooge's room with the appearance of the Ghost of Christmas Present.

And the description of the room seemed to be exactly the array of Christmas displays that Charles strove for in their own home.

Listening with a surprising new intensity, Kate found herself watching her husband more closely. He had always seen Christmas in a way that she hadn't originally. The entire world now knew of Charles Dickens's view of the season, but Kate had known it before the rest. The fervent decorating of their home. The elaborate feasts. The Christmas tree with all its adornments.

All of it was Charles and his love for Christmas. All of it was the Ghost of Christmas Present.

Perhaps, in all of this, Charles truly aimed to *be* that spirit of goodness and warmth and generosity.

Tears of love and pride filled the corners of her eyes as she watched him, as she listened, as she let herself feel her husband's deep love for the season. It was a beautiful, captivating, magical part of him that she so often took for granted. There was such power and joy in his vision of Christmas, and he had given all a glimpse into that world with his book.

## A Carol for Mrs. Dickens

She had seen the ripples that had spread upon its publication, and she could not deny that he might have succeeded in embodying that blessed Ghost of Christmas Present.

And she had the delight of being married to him.

"'Come in!' exclaimed the Ghost," Charles boomed in a deep, robust voice. "'Come in! and know me better, man!'"

Honestly, Kate could easily imagine Charles in a fine green robe or a mantle with white fur, such as what the ghost wore in the book, and felt the image rather apt.

Not feeling the need to stand quite as close to hear what she had heard several times before, Kate hedged toward the back of the gathered throng and pretended to see to the punch bowl and assortment of biscuits nearby.

Then she took a moment to survey the enraptured guests as they listened to Charles.

Her feelings were difficult to describe. Pleasure that their Christmas party had brought such smiles to their guests' faces. Pride that she had contributed in some way to their merriment. Hope that the rest of the evening would continue in much the same vein.

Envy was a startling contributor to the melee, however. Envious of their guests' new view of Christmas, thanks to Charles. Envious of their pure lightness and joy in this moment. Perhaps even envious of Charles himself and his passion for Christmas, let alone that he got to live in a world of characters and creations all his own.

*We take the good with the bad*, her younger self had told her.

She had felt her heart opening tonight, and in that moment, she willed it open further still.

She'd had fifteen years of marriage to Charles, and she still did not comprehend how he could be so brilliantly lit from within. His life prior to adulthood had been filled with dreadful experiences, things that would fill his books but no one would believe had filled his own existence, and yet he was laughing and dancing and celebrating Christmas with a full and cheerful heart. And he had shared that beautiful light of Christmas with the world in such a moving way.

## A Carol for Mrs. Dickens

Kate looked about the room, noting the excesses of greenery and ribbons, the Christmas tree with all its details, the gold-leafed fruit on display—all of it was for display alone. It was so much work and bother, and yet it soothed something in the soul, those decorations. They brightened the halls and lifted the spirits. Charles had known that long before Kate did, and their home had held such things from the very beginning of their marriage. Had she forgotten, in the many years of seeing them, how much good and light they gave to others?

It was a gift itself, she realized as she looked back at Charles. A gift so easily and readily given in a way that no one would refuse or even see as such. A gift to lift the spirits and lighten the heart, to beautify a space and bring a touch of magic and wonder into a gathering.

Charles was a giver of intangible gifts that could so easily be missed.

"Oh, dear Mrs. Dickens," Mrs. Montrose whispered loudly from her nearby chair, waving Kate to join her while Charles continued to read. "Just look at Miss Rutherford and Mr. Smythe. They are so in love, and to see such adoration at Christmas reminds me of my dear departed Stanley and myself when we were courting."

Kate hadn't given the engaged couple a moment of true notice before, but now she did so out of pure instinct. Miss Rutherford was a relation of Sir Walter Scott, whom Kate's father had worked with during Kate's childhood, and Mr. Smythe was an assistant in one of London's publishing firms, so it was a literary match of mutual admiration—and, as was clear to see from their close interactions and secret smiles, real affection, if not love.

Miss Rutherford was seven-and-twenty years of age, well-educated, and almost too tall for conventional beauty, but Mr. Smythe saw none of these things as a hindrance, judging by his constant smile and attention. He himself was a lanky fellow, near to thirty, and quick-witted, which made him a perfect match for her. A perfect match of interests, status, and affection.

"They should be very happy together," Kate murmured aloud, her thoughts wandering far from the particular couple before her.

On paper, they should have been very happy. But life tended to happen, good and bad, and everything changed.

Kate and Charles were no longer the giddy couple they had been in their courtship, of course. She had known that particular glow would fade the more settled they became, that it would mature just as they matured as individuals. They'd had nine children, and a tenth would soon be coming, and there was a deep, profound bond between them. A deeper, surer love. Something more binding and more complete. A love that could see them through the good and the bad in a way that the eager, giddy love could never do.

Kate was fairly certain she had a good marriage, all things considered. She did have a unique husband, but she had been raised to be a unique woman.

How could she have known that Christmas would

become so very important to their lives? Or had that been clear from the start?

Seeing that Charles was still engaged in his reading, Kate slipped out of the room and took refuge in her private parlor across the corridor.

She closed her eyes, the scent of pine and cinnamon filling the entire house room by room. And then she could suddenly see and feel the same bright, white light from before, making her skin tingle and her eyes squeeze more tightly shut. Everything was white and warm, almost painfully so, and all darkness was gone. The rushing sound filled her ears once more, and the floor beneath her feet disappeared.

Then, with the gentleness of a breath, her feet touched something solid, her ears were clear, and a cool breeze brushed across her face.

A lock of her hair danced along her brow and nose, and Kate reached up to push it back, her eyes opening with an almost reluctant wince.

Then they widened in shock as she gasped.

# CHAPTER 5

The view was one she was so familiar with that she could have drawn it from memory and done so with exactness.

Her parents' home in London, where they had finally settled after their stint in Yorkshire, where she had helped to tend her brothers and sisters, and the only home the twins, Helen and Edward, would ever be able to recall.

It was the house where she had dreamed of meeting a fine gentleman who would see her as his partner and equal. The very house she had been married from, and the place where she had penned so many heartsick letters to Charles when he had been too occupied with work and preparing to provide a home for them to see her.

If she was here and this was currently her family's home, it had to be 1834 at the earliest.

The brisk wind blew once more, and Kate shivered. The orchard trees were bare, and the gardens opposite the door were drab, so it must be winter.

"Of course," she whispered to herself, recollecting her previous experience. "It will be Christmastime."

But if this was Christmas at this particular location, then—

Kate put a hand to her mouth as the very familiar figure of a young man strode up the lane of number eighteen, his scarf jauntily thrown over his shoulder, and rapped firmly on the door.

Charles was coming to number eighteen.

She hadn't met him until 1835, and they'd been engaged that spring, though they would not marry until the spring following. So if he was calling upon her and it was Christmas . . .

They were currently engaged to be married.

She watched the door to number eighteen open

A CAROL FOR MRS. DICKENS

and her own much slimmer figure appear, bobbing a quick curtsey to Charles before throwing her arms around him. He swung her around like a twirling little girl, laughing heartily and kissing both her cheeks with perfunctory delight.

They started walking away from the house arm in arm, both talking quickly and eagerly, not paying any attention to the second figure exiting the house and falling into step behind them.

Kate, however, watched that second figure with a catch in her chest.

*Mary.*

Her younger sister, her first friend and confidante, had come to live with her and Charles in the early days of their marriage. She had passed away just a few months after Charley was born, collapsing without warning after they'd returned home from a play. It had been so wholly unexpected and a tragic upheaval of all their lives. Sweet, lighthearted Mary, as good a sister to both her and Charles as anyone could have wished for.

*81*

REBECCA CONNOLLY

Mamie had been born a mere eight months later and had been named for her.

Kate felt tears trickle down her face as she kept her eyes fixed on her sister, so healthy and hale, vibrant with anticipation for Kate's upcoming marriage and ready to take on the title of Miss Hogarth for her own rather than being Miss Mary as she had been all her life.

This memory was likely intended to be something more romantic, but Kate could not help but take a moment to soak up every sight of her departed sister with a fierce longing.

As though sensing eyes on her, Mary slowed a step and cast a sidelong glance in Kate's direction, but her gaze did not quite reach her.

Mary had always had a keen sense about what Kate needed and felt, so it was not the least bit surprising that she might feel an inkling of her presence.

The younger Kate, however, had no eyes or thoughts for anything but Charles. They were practically scampering toward the gardens and orchards, and following

## A Carol for Mrs. Dickens

the pair required more haste than Kate would have liked.

She remembered that eagerness, thought it seemed faint and far away in recollection. She had loved the giddiness that Charles made her feel, the engaging conversations that were so much more than the superficial ones she'd experienced with men before. It helped, of course, that Kate's father was Charles's employer and that Kate had been raised around literary works and literary artists, which had turned her into quite the avid reader as well as make her knowledgeable about the subject in general, but there had been a true connection with Charles in that shared love from the beginning.

His ambition had always been as clear as his talent, and, if she remembered right, at this time he had hopes on soon getting his name out into the wider world.

Everything would change once it did. For the better in most ways.

But as far as Kate could remember, Christmas had been more about church and helping the poor than anything else until more recently. So what was the

*83*

significance of this particular Christmas memory, and why had she been brought here?

She hurried along to catch up to herself and Charles, bewildered by the thought that she might have fallen in love with Christmas even a little bit so early in their relationship. Or had she simply fallen more in love with Charles and caught his eagerness for the holiday by association?

That seemed a far more plausible notion, but, again, she truly could not recall.

Life had filled her head with too many other memories, and this one had fallen by the wayside.

"I know there is a remarkable church service," Charles was saying as Kate reached the couple, "and it is my favorite one of the year as well, but Kate, there could be so much *more* to Christmas than just church."

"Christmas is the celebration of the birth of Christ," the young Kate reminded him with a disbelieving laugh. "Should we not focus on that?"

"Yes, of course!" Charles exhaled in exasperation, though still grinning at her. "But it should still be a cause for celebration! Families coming together and

## A Carol for Mrs. Dickens

sharing in the love and gratitude of the year and their lives. Giving to the less fortunate, not just a pittance that can be easily spared but graciously and generously, as our Lord did. Feasting with friends and reeling in the joy of the season! Do you know how celebratory this time of year has been throughout history, even before it was tied to Christianity?"

Young Kate, wide-eyed and captivated, nodded. "I have heard some of it, but surely you aren't suggesting a return to paganism."

"No, but why not bring their traditions in where they do not conflict with our own?" He gestured at the vacant trees around them. "We already do with the decorations of Christmas, bringing the greenery indoors when there is little to be found outside. That has pagan roots. It symbolizes the return of life itself in the spring and heralds goodwill for the coming year."

"I think I knew something of that," young Kate murmured, her blue eyes fixed on Charles. "But I do believe some have related the evergreen nature of it to the everlasting nature of Christ's love for us."

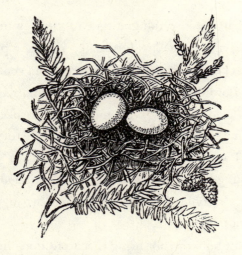

Charles was not perturbed in the least. "So it can have multiple meanings! Even more reason to celebrate!" He frowned in thought, looking around at the trees. "See here." He pointed up at a bare branch where a nest could be seen. "That nest is empty now, but it likely housed some precious cargo in the spring. Carefully constructed bit by bit, it becomes a place of safety for the nurturing care of the eggs. Once they are hatched, it becomes home and hearth until the chicks are big enough and strong enough to leave. Now it is empty and merely a bundle of twigs and bits, like all

## A Carol for Mrs. Dickens

these trees, once so magnificent and vibrant, but now without protection from the chill and the wind. It is enough to break any heart."

Kate smiled as she watched this younger version of herself stare at Charles in wonder, her astonishment at his passion and her fascination at how his mind worked evident in her features. No one had ever spoken with her the way Charles had, and his opinions were so clear, so strong, and so very much a central part of the man he was. His confidence and determination in whatever venture he undertook had always been attractive, but it was his vision of life and its meanings, shades, and shapes that had always drawn her in.

It also helped that he was a very handsome young man, but Kate had met plenty a handsome man who had been nothing more than an idiot.

Charles had been different.

"But there will come spring again," Charles went on with a quiet fervor, smiling gently at the empty nest. "And perhaps that small home will once again be used as a place of safety and nurturing."

"Spring will come again," his adoring young Kate said with a soft smile, shaking her head fondly. "What a beautiful reminder, Charles."

He actually appeared a little sheepish at that. "It is not my sentiment, my dear Pig."

Kate laughed, just as her younger self did. Charles had always called her the most unusual things in those days, mostly in letters but occasionally in conversation as well. She'd almost forgotten, but it was so delightfully creative and childlike that, in her mind, it had been an adorable expression of his feelings. Even now, the creative names he made up for the children were one of her favorite quirks of his.

"Holly and ivy and mistletoe all have ties to the custom of Yule," Charles went on with a trifle of red in his cheeks. "I cannot remember the exact details, but all were used for protection or to ward off evil. Winter was such a long, hard slog for our ancient ancestors that they needed to have the renewal of spring to look forward to. Why can we not celebrate that in conjunction with our more Christian traditions?"

A Carol for Mrs. Dickens

His adoring fiancée shook her head. "I don't know, Charles. Perhaps we should."

He looked at her quickly, a grin flashing across his features. "Perhaps *we* should. Kate, we can make Christmas whatever we like in our home. And we shall make it the grandest time of the year to celebrate all the good in our lives and to bring in the coming year with the best of luck."

"All right!" Kate exclaimed with a small laugh. "And we will give to the poor and the needy."

"Yes!" Charles came closer, setting his hands at her waist. "We will gather our friends and our family, especially our children, and celebrate with love and gratitude for all that we have, even when times are troubling."

Kate put her hands on his shoulders, gripping with the fervency of a woman in love. "And we will always have the greenery—the holly and rosemary and ivy and mistletoe."

Charles lifted her off the ground, spinning her again. "Especially the mistletoe!"

Squealing and giggling, Kate clung to him,

sighing when he set her to the ground. "Yes," she told him breathlessly. "Because spring will always come again."

"Always." Charles cupped her cheeks, leaning in to kiss her softly.

A sniffling sound met Kate's ears, and she realized it had come from herself. Her present self, so wrapped up in the beauty of this moment in her past, so long ago and lost in the midst of life, had forgotten she was only remembering such an encounter.

She swiped at her cheeks, damp with tears, and looked over at Mary, who had a small smile on her lips and had politely averted her eyes from the couple.

"We shall be those most peculiar Dickenses," the younger Kate mused after their kiss ended and Charles had moved his hands to hers. "The ones who exuberantly celebrate a holiday that others barely mention."

"All the better for us," Charles replied, shrugging his shoulders. "Perhaps we shall help the holiday to become more popular, if not more celebrated. I intend to spread goodwill and charity where I can, regardless of the time of year, but I think that Christmas might

## A Carol for Mrs. Dickens

be a time when others might be more inclined to do the same. We must never forget those who might observe the holiday and celebrate it with meager feasts and in humble dwellings, but who celebrate it nevertheless."

"Did not He who came for us all mark the first occasion in the most humble of dwellings?" young Kate asked in a rhetorical manner, nodding firmly at his sentiment. "And was He not given gifts by those with more to offer?"

"And did He not give the greatest gift of all?" Charles kissed Kate's gloved hands and started to walk with her again. "It all circles back on itself, Kate. Round and round in ever moving circles, and it all means that we should be celebrating with greater enthusiasm and joy."

"Also from scripture," Mary pointed out from behind the couple.

Charles looked behind his shoulder at her, his smile fond and warm, as it had always been for Kate's siblings. "Exactly so, Mary. Exactly."

Mary inclined her head in acknowledgment, maintaining her reserved, dignified composure.

"Wherever did you get your enthusiasm for Christmas, Charles?" young Kate asked him fondly.

"Oh, I don't know," he replied, returning his attention to her. "It's simply always held a special place in my heart. And then a few years ago I read 'A Visit from Saint Nicholas.' Do you know it?"

Kate felt her heart skip a beat and her body still as the remembered moment flashed through her mind with perfect clarity, just as she was seeing it now with her eyes. No longer lost but renewed and now to be forever treasured.

"Yes, though I cannot recall any lines of it," she heard her younger self admit with a laugh.

As if he had been waiting for such an invitation, Charles cleared his throat and struck a pose.

> *'Twas the night before Christmas,*
> *and all through the house,*
> *not a creature was stirring,*
> *not even a mouse.*

## A Carol for Mrs. Dickens

For the next few minutes, both Kates, as well as Mary, listened to Charles recite the poem, expertly altering his voice for each character and using every ounce of dramaticism he possessed to bring the scene to life.

It was a beloved poem in Kate's present and had been a favorite of all the Dickens children as they had grown. For years, Kate had been unable to recall where the love and delight for that specific poem had come from, yet here was the genesis of its tradition within their family.

Charles had loved it, known it, and treasured it, then shared it with her and with their children. The world would eventually adore it just as much, but Charles had loved it earlier.

Just as he had with Christmas. And he had shared that love with them. That joy and desire to celebrate in a time of year when hope and light and love were needed most.

Kate had seen that in him and fallen in love with Christmas through her love for him. It had been one of the things that had struck her most in their relationship.

How had she forgotten?

> *But I heard him exclaim*
> *'Ere he drove out of sight:*
> *"Happy Christmas to all!*
> *And to all a good night!"*

Charles finished the poem with a deep, booming voice that seemed to echo throughout the trees. Then he sighed deeply and bowed to his small audience.

Young Kate and Mary applauded merrily. "What a thrilling performance, Charles!" Kate praised, clasping her hands beneath her chin. "I may have you do the same every Christmas!"

Charles grinned. "And I may indulge you every Christmas." He turned to her sister. "Mary, shall we go find some less fortunate folk to spread Christmas cheer to? What say you?"

"Oh, I would love to," Mary said and started walking beside him back toward their home with the still-delighted Kate following at a slower pace, her attention wholly on Charles.

Kate took the opportunity to walk beside herself,

# A Carol for Mrs. Dickens

hoping she might be able to have the moment with her that she had with the previous memory.

Sure enough, her young self met her eyes as soon as she arrived. "He is so wonderful, isn't he? So vibrant and alive!"

"He does have that effect on people," Kate replied as she took in the trim figure of her young husband.

"I am by no means ignorant of his flaws, you know." The younger Kate shook her head firmly. "I am well aware of his obsession with his stories and his determination to work himself to death over his writing. Believe me, I have begged him to be less so and to spend more time with me. It was not a pleasant response, if you will recall."

Kate did not recall, but the almost smug look on her younger face amused her. "What? Why do you look like that if he gave you an unpleasant response?"

"Because I love him anyway," came the simple response. "We do, I mean. We never expected a perfect man, Kate. We were raised to be a cultured, well-read, freethinking woman, and this is a man who loves culture, is well-read, and . . . well, he is freethinking. I cannot yet say what he will make of my thinking." She laughed with surprising ease. "But we adore him and the way he experiences life. There is such joy in him and with him, and we will see the whole world through him, even if we never leave England's shores."

"What if it's hard?" Kate asked in a low voice. "Harder and more challenging than we ever imagined?"

Young Kate shrugged, a content smile on her lips. "Even better. There is nowhere I would rather be than where he is. I can be happy anywhere with him, I firmly believe. And I will be."

Kate wanted to tell her that she was wrong, that she would not always be happy, that she was destined for some truly hard and heartrending things, but she could not bring herself to destroy the youthful bliss.

"How can you be so certain?" she asked instead.

Her younger self met her eyes, knowledge, understanding, and compassion in their blue depths. "Because I am determined to be. I do not believe this giddiness will last, but I believe that my own happiness is

A Carol for Mrs. Dickens

a choice. And I choose it with him." She put a hand on Kate's arm, squeezing gently, then strode away, hurrying to catch up with Charles and Mary.

Kate watched her go, wondering at the wisdom of her young self and if she had truly held such convictions then.

She exhaled slowly and let her eyes fall shut, the impossible darkness returning and the tugging at her waist and shoulders prying her from the memory and the ground beneath her feet.

# CHAPTER 6

This time, Kate was not surprised to find herself returned to her parlor, knowing it would again only have been a few moments that she was away.

But it had been enough.

Her heart was still so tender, so filled with appreciation for her husband's view of the world and reasoning for celebrating at Christmas. And there was a calmness to her now that she had not previously felt. Some inner peace that she had been seeking for ages. It was not a healing feeling, so to speak, nor could she admit that all had been made whole, but there was a gentle reassurance that all would be well enough.

REBECCA CONNOLLY

*My own happiness is a choice.*

She could choose to be happy regardless of her circumstances.

It would take time, but even the certainty that one day she *could* find it made her even more hopeful that it would be true.

She could choose for it to be true.

Smiling at the greenery that had made its way into her parlor, Kate shook her head. "Spring will come again," she murmured softly.

Her heart seemed to swell with warmth and pride as she left the room, crossing back to the drawing room.

The guests were still gathered before Charles, fixed upon his figure.

"Then Bob proposed: 'A Merry Christmas to us all, my dears. God bless us!'" Charles intoned in his best reading voice, being sure to give his dear Bob Cratchit enough of a common accent to befit the character but not so much as to make him low.

He was only at the end of his passage of reading, which meant Kate had been gone only a matter of minutes, hardly enough to even bear notice.

*100*

## A Carol for Mrs. Dickens

What a remarkable, peculiar thing!

Entering the room fully, Kate stood along the wall to watch the finale of the reading.

"Which," Charles went on, narrating now, "all the family re-echoed. 'God bless us every one!' said Tiny Tim, the last of all."

Closing the book with a sharp snap, Charles swept it behind his back, inclining his head.

Applause erupted from the room, most of the seated guests rising to their feet and cheering as loudly as though they were in a theater. Charles bowed, just as he had in the memory she had visited.

Still touched by the experience, Kate found tears at the ready and applauded along with the rest. For him. For his spirit. For his influence. For his goodness.

For the holly, rosemary, mistletoe, evergreen, and all the rest of the beauty he had brought into their house, and their lives, to celebrate Christmas.

That was most certainly worth applauding.

"Shall we have some carols now?" Charles asked over the din of the applause, his smile almost wild

*101*

with the building energy. "Come, back to the schoolroom! Let us sing!"

While no one could possibly match him for enthusiasm, the guests certainly tried their best to follow him with all speed and eagerness.

The musicians were still there, having been engaged to play for the entire length of the evening, and stood nearly to attention while Charles spoke with them.

One moved to the pianoforte and began to play as Charles cleared his throat, waving everyone in, either to chairs or to stand by the wall.

"*I care not for spring; on his fickle wing*," Charles sang in a surprisingly deep, rather common accent. "*Let the blossoms and buds be borne.*"

A few of the guests began to laugh, and even Kate found herself snickering softly.

Charles was singing his own carol. Something he had written for his first literary venture and love, *The Pickwick Papers*, and it wasn't often brought out, even for parties.

Tonight, apparently, he was acting out the part of the old miner and singing his carol for the crowd.

## A Carol for Mrs. Dickens

It was a very Charles thing to do and would certainly provide entertainment enough for their guests. Perhaps by starting the singing himself, he could remove any embarrassment others might feel in doing the same, especially by offering up such a silly carol. Even Charles had admitted it was not a great piece of poetry, even when put to music, but it was festive and jolly, which was undoubtedly the point.

But it was also about Christmas itself, its celebration and seasonal fervor, and Kate, her mind full of memories of gifts and decorations, found herself longing for a moment of simplicity. A moment to remember what was at the heart of the holiday.

If they were to sing for a while, Kate could take a few more minutes away from the room and guests without being missed.

Between the overwhelming memories she was reliving, the heat of the fireplace, the crowding of the house, and the loud laughter and singing, she found herself more than a touch overwhelmed. They were all good and wonderful things, but with them all rushing in on her at once, she could use a reprieve.

A brief step into the cool night air would allow her a restorative respite to see her through the rest of the evening.

Kate slipped out of the schoolroom and out to the landing, smiling when she saw Mrs. Morley once more, this time with a tea tray in her hands. "What are you up to now, Mrs. Morley?"

"A bit of warm chocolate for your young'uns, madam," she replied cheerily. "The older ones, mind. I know well the babbies will be sleeping."

Smiling softly, Kate nodded. "Yes, they will." She leaned against the wall a little, fanning her warm face. "I needed to get away from everything for a moment. I thought I might step outside and get some cool air."

"An evening walk, madam?" Mrs. Morley nodded in approval. "Just the ticket, I think. One does not often get a quiet moment to appreciate Christmas Eve, eh? Go for a stroll, I say. All will be well here for a few minutes, for certain."

Kate rubbed her stomach absently. "I took many evening walks after we lost Dora. It helped me to feel closer to her and to align my thoughts." She trailed off,

## A Carol for Mrs. Dickens

remembering those dark yet precious days, noting how the sting of that memory was much less than before.

That alone was a miracle.

"Apologies," Kate said with a quick clearing of her throat as she waved at Mrs. Morley. "You are very kind to listen to me rattle on when you've an errand and a tray in your hands. Please, do go on. And thank you for your kindness. The children will love it."

"Aye, madam, I do hope so." Mrs. Morley started up the stairs and looked over her shoulder. "Do take a stroll, madam. It will do you good."

Kate watched her go with a touch of fondness. She hadn't thought of taking a full walk, only a few moments to breathe, but the idea of a lingering stroll while her guests were pleasantly occupied would be a gift in and of itself for Christmas Eve.

She moved up to her room to fetch a cloak, then hurried back down the stairs and out the front door. Inhaling deeply, she reveled in the feeling of cold air filling her lungs, tickling the edges and giving a revitalizing energy to her entire body. She could not go far, as her cheeks and nose would certainly turn quite pink if she tarried too long in the chill, but a short walk would not go at all amiss.

The sky was perfectly clear, and the stars were utterly brilliant in the inky blackness beyond. It was a captivating sight on this particular Christmas Eve, enough to slow her step and turn her pace to something quite meandering.

What had the sky looked like in Bethlehem that first Christmas? Had there been clouds or stars? Had Mary even noticed the sky in her pain and fear over the impending delivery of her first child? She would have been so young and her situation so precarious; she knew who her son would be and of the prophecies concerning Him, but how much did she really know?

Had she thought of the promises in scripture when He kicked inside her? When she had looked at her boy on the cross, had her mind gone back to the night of His birth? Had she remembered cradling Him for the first time and wrapping Him in those swaddling clothes? When she handed the baby to Joseph, had she wondered how she could do any of this?

Or had God given Mary all the strength, all the

## A CAROL FOR MRS. DICKENS

peace, all the comfort, and all the assurance she could have needed at that moment and beyond?

Kate put her hand to the swell of her stomach, feeling the tumbling of her child within her, imagining him stretching and moving to try to find a more comfortable position. There would be even less room the more the baby grew. Who would this child be? Who would they become? What would they add to the world?

Would God give her some semblance of Mary's certainty if Kate asked for it?

She was not the same woman she had been at the beginning of the evening—her memory visits had unlocked something in her heart that had long been closed—but she was not quite ready to claim a victory or anything so miraculous. She felt a beautiful reassurance in her children and her husband and everything that Christmas with them had brought into her life. So what else did she need? What else could help her tonight?

Was there anywhere else in her past that she could even imagine going?

That was a ridiculous question. As if she had been directing any of these memory visitations or had any control over where she went or how long she stayed there. Whatever power was allowing these extraordinary experiences for her had its own agenda as to the curriculum of the night's lessons, and Kate was simply the student.

The sound of scuffling feet brought Kate's attention down from the sky to the street, and she scanned her surroundings quickly.

Scarcely a block ahead of her were two small children walking hand in hand.

It was far too late for children to be out and about, and on Christmas Eve? It was absolutely unthinkable. Kate quickened her pace, determined to catch up to them. Were they all right? Where were they going? Why were they out so late? Did they have some place warm to go on Christmas Eve?

If she did not receive satisfactory answers to those questions, she would take them home with her and see them adequately warmed and fed. Once the holiday was observed, she would then see about finding them

## A Carol for Mrs. Dickens

suitable lodging and living situations, if they had none in place.

It only took a few additional steps for her to recognize them, even from behind.

The children were the brother and sister she had seen on the corner in the market that morning, selling sprigs of holly. The clothing was worn but seemed sturdy enough, and certainly the layers bore the appropriate thickness for the cold London winter. But it was still too cold and too late for them to be out and about.

Yet they were taking determined steps, neither pulling each other nor resisting. They seemed to be walking a well-known path based on their pace and their demeanor.

Not wanting to frighten them, Kate kept her distance now, content to wait and concerned enough to watch with care.

They went a few blocks more, weaving this way and that, leading Kate into the defiantly poorer parts of the neighborhood, as she had anticipated.

What she had *not* anticipated was the music that

seemed to come from every part of the street they were on. The windows of each home were filthy, but light glowed from behind them all the same. In fact, the film of grime somehow made the light seem gentle and more welcoming. The faint bit of snow on the ground, tucked into the random corners of buildings and rooftops, added a sweet and festive scene in a place where Kate had least expected it.

It was Christmas Eve here as well, and the reminder was apt as well as humbling.

Kate watched as the children moved to the poorest, dankest part of the street and pushed aside a stack of crates to open a door almost hidden in the shadows. She couldn't hear any sounds from within given her present position, but she moved to the window, hoping there was someone at home to welcome the children.

A kind-faced young woman sat beside a weak fire, heavily pregnant and struggling to rise from her chair. She gestured for them to come over and hugged each child tightly. She picked a plate up from near the fire and handed it to the children. The children sat on the

A CAROL FOR MRS. DICKENS

floor before their mother and began to eat the small pies eagerly.

Some jaunty whistling reached Kate's ears, and she ducked behind the crates, suddenly recollecting that she was not currently in a memory and thus visible to everyone.

Through the slats of the crates, Kate could see a man in a flat cap and thin scarf reaching the door to the house. When he entered, the children raced to him with a cry of delight and were swept up into his arms.

"Merry Christmas, my loves! How did you do today?" the man asked, shutting the door behind him.

Kate peeped through the window again, heart pounding in the very tips of her fingers.

The boy showed his father their money, and his hair was ruffled proudly. "Well done, my boy! I've had a rather good day meself, and as such . . ." He reached into his pockets and pulled out two oranges, handing one to each child.

Their squeals of excitement were beautiful sounds, and Kate's eyes filled with tears as the children sat by the fire and began to peel their oranges. The man

*111*

moved to his wife and pulled a third orange from his pocket, setting it in her lap before pressing a soft kiss to her brow.

Kate watched a few minutes more as the father pulled a peculiarly carved wooden figure from a sack, set it down beside him, then removed another and began whittling away at it. She looked more closely, trying to determine what he was creating.

It was the figure of a child in a cradle of sorts.

She looked at the figure he had set down and recognized it as a sheep. Her breath caught, and her eyes darted to the one in his hand.

*A manger.*

He was carving a nativity, and, looking at the sack on the floor beside him, she could see other figures in there as well. Had he completed the set? Was he just beginning? She could not know and could not inquire, but this sweet family who had so very little celebrated Christmas by being together, giving small gifts, and focusing on the beautiful truths at the center of the day.

And that was Christmas enough for them.

## A Carol for Mrs. Dickens

Covering her mouth, both to stifle tears and to warm her fingers, Kate moved away from the tiny but love-filled home and made her way back toward her own.

The party at Tavistock House would continue a bit longer, but she would not soon forget this simple, beautiful Christmas sight, nor what it meant to her.

Her thoughts were far from home as she walked, pondering the village of Bethlehem, the music of the street she had just departed, and the possible ways she could help the family she had just seen. It was a medley of thoughts, really, interweaving with each other without finding any specific action or purpose for herself. It was a veritable tableau of images and sounds in her mind, almost like a dream, taking all

awareness from her steps and leaving her route to pure instinct.

Echoes of the carolers singing from earlier in the day returned to her mind, melodies of "The Holly and the Ivy" mingling with "Hark! The Herald Angels Sing" and the sounds of sleigh bells. She could almost smell the hot wine, cinnamon, oranges, and pine again. The dark streets were almost bright with candles and roaring fires and glistening chandeliers reflecting every glimmer of light this way and that. It was a gorgeous array, and she sensed that, somehow, she had missed it before. Had seen it without really noticing much, and it was a bittersweet realization.

She would not miss more.

Somehow, she had returned to Tavistock House minutes later and tossed her cloak on a divan in the room just off the entry. She'd see to it later, when she had more clarity of thought and did not have a party to contend with.

The musicians had struck up again, if the sounds from above were any indication, and there was un-doubtedly more dancing still to happen. What carols

## A Carol for Mrs. Dickens

had the partygoers sung while she had been away? What merriment had taken place? Could any of it have moved her more than what she had just witnessed in an overlooked portion of London?

Likely not, but it would all serve to lift the hearts of their guests just the same. Charles loved a good laugh, and she adored that about him. She had no doubt the guests had fed off his energy and sung whatever silly or robust carols he suggested. She hoped, however, that there might have also been some of the more traditional carols as well, just to give them all a touch of remembrance for what was at the heart of this day.

Making her way back to the schoolroom, hoping her cheeks were not too rosy from the cold, Kate found her plate of biscuits where she had left it. She picked it up and began to make her way around the room once more, asking any who were watching the dancing if they would like a biscuit or any other refreshment.

Then she set the plate aside and began to truly mingle, sitting beside some of the ladies and gentlemen to discuss anything that came to mind. Any topic was suitable at this point, and their positivity had an influence on her. Her smile became easy and natural, her fatigue lessened, and she felt something gentle and quiet rest within her heart. She found her own laughter at hand, and a hint of relaxation touched her shoulders and her frame while every glance about the room seemed to fill her more and more with happiness.

That was certainly progress, and she would accept it with open arms.

And, she prayed, a further opening heart.

She could feel these changes within her and marveled at them. It had become so impossibly easy to exist from day to day without engaging her heart, especially in her grief over the loss of Dora. Somehow, that had extended to Christmas, and she had been afraid to let herself recall the joy and the hope and the spirit of this glorious season.

She was being given a gift tonight in reliving these memories. A wonderous, magical gift to bring Christmas back to her in all its generosity, beauty, frivolity, and delight. And with that sweet family she had just

A CAROL FOR MRS. DICKENS

seen, she had also been given the reminder of how powerful the simplicity of love at Christmas could be.

Dancing went on for at least another hour, a whirl of country dances, jigs, reels, and even waltzes on display for all to see. The dancers' energy never waned, and the guests watching seemed to enjoy the experience, offering plenty of whooping, clapping, and foot stamping, and even a few whistles to accompany the music and dancing, raising the feeling of celebration higher still.

If any of the Dickens children could sleep through this, Kate would be astonished.

Finally, Charles called for the final dance—the Sir Roger de Coverley country dance. "It's what I have the Fezziwigs do," he assured the group with a smile.

That was encouragement enough for all of them.

The delightful country dance was soon over, and everyone was sighing and groaning at the evening's entertainment being forced to end.

"Come, come, everyone," Charles insisted, waving the group back toward the drawing room. "Come admire the Christmas tree before you depart and take

REBECCA CONNOLLY

something else home with you. We insist, we absolutely insist. Please, come." He gestured wildly and hurried toward the room as the guests began to follow.

Kate hung back, going over to the musicians and thanking them for their playing that evening. "Please, do see the Christmas tree for yourselves," she offered, "and take something home. Then be sure to leave by way of the kitchens. I am certain Mrs. Rook will have a meal prepared for you."

"Thank you, madam," they replied with scattered appreciation.

She nodded and slowly made her way to the drawing room. Charles was by the Christmas tree, showing it off as though it were one of their children, and handing items from the tree to guests like he was Father Christmas. Some of the guests waved to Kate as they were leaving. Charles was much too occupied to notice at first, but Kate made sure to wave back.

Then Charles *did* notice and almost scampered from the space with the next round of guests, accompanying them downstairs and prattling on about the tree or the meal or what their plans were for Christmas Day.

## A Carol for Mrs. Dickens

Sooner than she expected, Kate was alone in the drawing room, letting her smile ease into relaxation with a slow exhale and feeling her shoulders sag with relief. She would sleep well tonight; that was absolutely certain. There was only so much energy one could give to others before the energy for the following day began to be taken up as well.

But with their eight active children on Christmas Day, she was not likely to have much rest tomorrow.

She could manage that for Christmas, couldn't she?

In fact, the part of Christmas that was just for her family was the part she looked forward to the most. Yes, there was fun in the merriment and celebrations, in gifts and decorations, but the true heart of Christmas, in Kate's mind, was family. Her children and Charles. Her parents, even, and her siblings. Christmas felt most like Christmas when she was with family.

And when one spoke of Christmas, there was, at its core, a very small and very new family that made it all possible.

*119*

Kate took a moment to look at the stunning Christmas tree, finding a true smile for it. Charles really had outdone himself. Her eyes moved to the fire, and she stood there for a long moment, seeing nothing and simply allowing the warmth to envelop her while the popping and crackling sounds soothed her heart.

The chimes from the mantel clock began to ring, and Kate closed her eyes, breathing in and out with the sounds of the room in the quiet space.

To her surprise, the warmth she felt began to spread and increase, the bright, white light sneaking through her closed eyelids, and the tingling, tugging sensation taking her from the present yet again.

# CHAPTER 7

There were still chimes sounding somewhere.

Kate blinked quickly, clearing the brightness from her vision, realizing at once that she was in a fairly bright place. Light streamed in from tall windows, and the massive space had rows and rows of people sitting with their backs to her.

And still there were chimes. Distant ones, but still . . .

No, she realized. Not chimes. Bells.

From outside, bells were ringing.

As she looked around, taking stock of her position, she began to recognize the space she was in, and a wild grin spread across her lips.

She stood in Greyfriars Kirk in Edinburgh, at the back of the hall, facing the pulpit along with everyone gathered there. This was the church her family had attended when she was a child. This was the church she had been christened in.

This was where she had spent Christmas services as a child.

And if she was here now . . .

Kate bit her lip as she looked around the pews, inhaling sharply and feeling tears in her eyes when she recognized the figures of her mother and father, as well as her younger siblings, sitting in one of the middle pews. Her mother was shushing one of Kate's brothers, as was to be expected.

Then the little girl sitting at the far end turned around and looked right at Kate, her familiar bright-blue eyes filled with happiness, hope, and a hint of impishness. She grinned and offered her a little wave, giggling just a little.

Kate waved back, just a little.

Her mother indicated that little Kate turn to face the pulpit as the minister rose to speak.

## A Carol for Mrs. Dickens

"The voice of God summons us to worship," he intoned in his deep, rolling brogue. "Prepare the way of the Lord. On this morning of all mornings, we turn our faces and our voices toward heaven and invite the merciful presence of our Lord to be here among us. Let us raise our voices in gratitude, humility, and joyful celebration of spirit as befitting that of Christmas Day."

Kate walked forward, her heart lifting in this familiar place, a childlike thrill of delight racing through her body like its own special fire. She took a seat a few pews behind and to the side of her family, tracing the shape of each of them, not entirely certain of the year she was visiting but knowing each of the sweet faces she saw as intimately as she knew her own.

She flat-out ignored the prayers of the minister as she marveled at her mother's youthful face, her father's hair that bore not a hint of gray, Robert's ruddy face and frequent fidgeting, and Mary's inability to whisper. And that little boy peering over the pew in her direction must be little George.

Kate shook her head as she stared into his sweet face. He could not have been more than a year in age.

Her mother would either be carrying William at this time or shortly would be. Kate would be perhaps six or seven years of age, which was right when her heart had begun to treasure up the more spiritual things in life.

What a perfect time to see and hear and feel the Christmas she had grown up with in all its simple beauty.

A small choir in plain robes rose near the pulpit and began to sing, the purity in their voices ringing from every corner of the massive space.

"*Of the Father's Love Begotten*," they began in almost haunting tones, unison for now. "'*Ere the world began to be. He is Alpha and Omega, He the source, the ending He . . .*"

Kate could not recall a more stirring moment of music in her entire life, and she had been to several operas and concerts in her present. But there was nothing like this simple, unadorned choir in its ancient church in Scotland, singing its loving praises on this Christmas morning. The light through the windows seemed to shine even brighter, the chill of the winter outside seemed to fade, the cares and concerns

## A Carol for Mrs. Dickens

of her life seemed to diminish, and her soul seemed to reach for heaven itself, straining against her mortal constraints.

The choir eventually shifted their voices into a harmony, and the ethereal nature of the hymn was even more pronounced. It was a solemn song of praise, but solemn did not have to mean dreary. The poignancy of the hymn's message was all the more notable for its lack of frills and trills, and the clarity in the tone of the singers was such that every word held weight. Yet the notes upon which those words were carried seemed as light as the air they filled.

The hymn flew on wings all its own, the music strengthening every one of the listeners as well as the singers. There was power and spirit in every movement in the melody and in the expressions of everyone singing.

Joy in every note, in every word, in every breath required to raise these praises.

This was Christmas. This simple, poignant beauty, so understated and underappreciated, that captivated

REBECCA CONNOLLY

the heart and mind in ways that could not be denied and could barely be expressed.

The song was soon finished, and the minister rose once more.

"From the Gospel of St. Luke," he said with an adjustment of his spectacles, "in the second chapter. 'And she brought forth her firstborn son, and wrapped him in swaddling clothes, and laid him in a manger; because there was no room for them in the inn. And there were in the same country shepherds abiding in the field, keeping watch over their flock by night. And, lo, the angel of the Lord came upon them, and the glory of the Lord shone round about them: and they were sore afraid. And the angel said unto them, Fear not: for, behold, I bring you good tidings of great joy, which shall be to all people. For unto you is born this day in the city of David a Saviour, which is Christ the Lord. And this shall be a sign unto you; Ye shall find the babe wrapped in swaddling clothes, lying in a manger. And suddenly there was with the angel a multitude of the heavenly host praising God, and saying, Glory to God

## A Carol for Mrs. Dickens

in the highest, and on earth peace, good will toward men.'"

He raised his eyes and looked around at the congregation. "This is the message of this day. He has come to bring good tidings of great joy, and so we must live the good tidings of great joy. We must give glory to God and fill the earth with peace, giving goodwill to all men."

Kate found herself nodding as she listened, as did everyone else in the congregation, including her family. Her young self was nodding very quickly, and Kate laughed to herself at the eagerness in the action.

"And from the book of Isaiah," the minister went on, clearing his throat, "in the ninth chapter, we hear these wonderful prophecies: 'The people that walked in darkness have seen a great light: they that dwell in the land of the shadow of death, upon them hath the light shined. Thou hast multiplied the nation, and not increased the joy: they joy before thee according to the joy in harvest, and as men rejoice when they divide the spoil. For thou hast broken the yoke of his burden, and the staff of his shoulder, the rod of his oppressor, as in the day of Midian. For every battle of the warrior is with confused noise, and garments rolled in blood; but this shall be with burning and fuel of fire. For unto us a child is born, unto us a son is given: and the government shall be upon his shoulder: and his name shall be called Wonderful, Counsellor, The mighty God, The everlasting Father, The Prince of Peace. Of the increase of his government and peace there shall be no end, upon the throne of David, and upon his kingdom, to order it, and to establish it with judgment and with justice from henceforth even for ever. The zeal of the Lord of hosts will perform this.'"

He paused there, shaking his head as he looked out at the congregants. "The zeal of the Lord of hosts. What a promise for us, and what a word to choose for a promise. Do we have the zeal of the Lord of hosts in our hearts this day? As we walk in the darkness of life, have we seen the great light He brings? Do we feel the wonder in this prophecy being fulfilled: a child was born, a Son was given, and He was, and is, the Everlasting Prince of Peace."

Kate's soul swelled as she listened to the words,

## A Carol for Mrs. Dickens

as her mind took in the scripture, as she recognized the beauty in the messages, as her heart softened and warmed, as her tears began to flow.

This was what she had been missing. Gifts and decorations and parties were lovely, but *this* was the source of her true joy and peace at Christmas.

*This* was what she needed.

The choir rose again, this time singing "Whilst Shepherds Watched Their Flocks by Night," and Kate put her hand to her heart, shaking her head in disbelief.

How could she possibly have forgotten a memory so potent, so powerful, so tenderly moving to the soul?

The answer, of course, was simple: She had been a child at the time. While she might have appreciated the sermon and the music for what it was, the true meaning and significance could not possibly have touched her in the same way then. It could be the foundation upon which many things were built, but the memory in its purity would be lost among many other sermons, many other songs, and the busy business of life itself.

The reminder of this experience now awakened

parts of Kate's soul that she had thought long gone, the parts she had thought lost, the parts she had so tearfully sought without knowing the exact nature of them.

Her little self glanced over the pew at her, smiling the knowing smile of a much older woman, those innocent, bright eyes filled now with sympathy and love. It was as though she could see the life Kate had led thus far in its entirety and she knew how much this memory meant and was needed at this very moment. Even this child could sense the truth and the power, the very impact this memory would have on Kate, and knew that this would help her move forward to whatever new memories lay ahead. Whatever the future held for Kate or for any of her family, this memory visitation would be the one that would matter most. This was at the very heart of who Catherine Dickens was as a woman, not just as a mother or a wife but who she truly was and had ever hoped to become.

This was the heart of her Christmas.

It always had been.

Such beauty and such peace. She had sought those

## A Carol for Mrs. Dickens

feelings for so many months now, perhaps even years, and here they were in her memories. In truths so rooted in her core that she could probably have found them if she had looked deeply enough. But perhaps it had been too many years for such a discovery to be made under her own willpower. Perhaps she needed something extraordinary to come to such a realization. Perhaps the very reason these visits had happened to her was because of the depth to which such beauty and truth had been buried.

It was a miracle she was here, experiencing these important memories again. Utterly unbelievable but for the fact that it was real and she could not deny it. No one would believe her, but no one had to. These were moments from her past, and to visit them again was no one's business but her own. This was nothing to proclaim to the world but something to treasure up in her heart and cling to for the rest of her life.

This was the promised whisper of Christmas magic that had tingled at the edges of the entire night.

The rest of the service passed in a blur to Kate, filled with rises and falls, smiles and tears, and moments where she just watched her parents and her siblings, as well as herself, enjoy the service together.

When the service concluded, the choir singing a lovely recessional hymn to accompany their departure from the church, Kate waited for her family to pass her on the way out before following. She wanted a little more time with them, could not bear to sever the ties with this memory so soon.

She followed her family on the familiar walk from Greyfriars to their home, the snow piled up along the walkways and the cold biting at their cheeks and noses. But the day was sunny and the feeling so jubilant that none of them seemed to notice. Bells rang out all over the city of Edinburgh, adding a heavenly anthem to the day. How long had it been since Kate had appreciated the bells that rang out on Christmas Day from all the services across town?

The family crossed the street, and the two little ones walked right by a man in tattered clothing sitting at the corner, his face, hands, and feet covered with dirt and soot. He was unbelievably gaunt and seemed

## A CAROL FOR MRS. DICKENS

weighed down by some invisible boulder upon his shoulders.

Kate watched as her father immediately removed his thick, woolen scarf from around his neck and stooped to meet the man's eyes.

"Here," she heard him murmur. "You've more need of it than I."

The poor man stared at the scarf for a moment, then met her father's eyes in wonder. "Sir?"

Her father wrapped it about the man's shoulders without hesitation. "It's only going to get colder, you know. And my wife made this, so you can be assured of the quality. It will be just the thing to fend off the worst of the chill."

"Sir, I cannot—"

"Of course you can," he broke in gently but firmly. "It is Christmas." He rose and nodded in satisfaction. "And it is an excellent color for you."

The man fingered the edges of the scarf tenderly, tears trickling down his cheeks. "God bless you, sir."

"And you. Merry Christmas." He took his wife's arm and continued up the street toward their home.

"Papa, do you know him?" young Kate inquired with an innocent skip to her step.

"No, Kate. But God does."

It took Kate a long moment to realize that she was crying, let alone that she was no longer following her family. She simply looked between the bewildered homeless man and her father, wondering how such a memory had ever left her mind.

Her father had not planned the meeting, had not made any sort of grand proclamation about doing good and then arranging to act in such a way for his children's benefit. He simply acted. He simply saw a need and filled it. All because he could.

She had no memory of this Christmas or this lesson of her father's, but she felt rather tenderly attached to it now. This was the heart of everything that was Christmas, and she so wished she could remain and linger in the quiet goodness of this particular day.

Still, time was not infinite for her, and she had a present to return to.

Her little-girl self stopped on her way home and looked back at Kate for a long moment. Then she smiled again, a remarkable amount of reassurance in the curve of such a small mouth. With a quick wave, she followed her parents and siblings up the street, disappearing from sight.

Kate waved as well, though no one would see it now. That did not matter. She was waving farewell to this memory as much as to her very young self. Farewell to the sermon and music in the church. Farewell to the bells in Edinburgh. Farewell to the lesson of her father's giving heart.

Farewell to this particular Christmas.

Sighing very softly, Kate closed her eyes, the impossible darkness of departure taking over her eyelids, the ground falling away beneath her feet, and the tugging sensation prying her from this moment.

One last time.

# Chapter 8

he fire still crackled in the grate, but the chiming of the clock had stopped.

Kate stared at the flames for several long moments, letting everything she had experienced wash over her in waves of sensation and memory, knowing it would take time to process it all. She did not need to understand everything now; she simply needed to feel.

And she felt warmth, peace, and, impossibly, joy.

Not a giddy happiness that made her wish the party would continue but a quiet contentedness that surpassed anything else. Something deeper and purer, something sturdy enough for a foundation and enduring enough for a life.

Remarkably, at this moment, Kate felt the most like herself than she had in years.

What a blessed Christmas Eve this had been! What an experience to be reminded not only of the beauty of Christmas but also the beauty of her own life and her own memories.

She could choose to continue on and to find joy where it existed. In her love for her children, her love for her husband, and her love for the Lord. There was so much good amid all the other noise and chaos, and she had only to take the time to find it. To remember it was there. To give herself the grace and understanding that she would give to others and to reach into her deepest reserves for what had seen her through other difficult times and passages of her life.

Even at Christmas.

Especially at Christmas.

She could take the good with the bad. Spring would come again. The Lord had come.

Good tidings of great joy, indeed.

She heard Charles coming up the stairs, his steps a trifle trudging compared to his former levels of energy.

A CAROL FOR MRS. DICKENS

"Kate?" he called from the stairs.

"Here," she returned, turning from the fire in anticipation.

He came to the doorway and leaned against the frame, his smile tired but wide. "Another successful year."

"Indeed. And another party to come at Twelfth Night." She laughed softly, finding no resentment to the statement now.

"Do you hate being married to such a party enthusiast?" he asked her, laughing as well.

Kate shook her head and started toward him with a smile, feeling not the giddy, girlish love she'd witnessed earlier but a deep, thriving, enduring love that was so much more. "No. I love being married to a man so enthusiastic and passionate. And who else would make certain we have such a splendid Christmas tree every year?"

Charles extended a hand to her, and she took it, lacing their fingers together. He brought it to his lips for a tender kiss, then looked at the tree. "It is rather splendid, isn't it?"

Kate snorted a soft laugh, nodding her head. "Yes, it is."

"We'd better put out the tapers before we go up," he said on a sigh. "The children will want to help light them in the morning."

"They will," Kate agreed, walking with him across the room. Together, they began dousing the almost mystical light that the tapers on the tree provided.

After that was completed, they started toward the stairs together, heading toward their bedchamber for the night.

"Charles," Kate said slowly as her thoughts began to form some sort of cohesion from the night she'd had. "About tomorrow morning."

"Yes?"

She met his eyes and offered a smile. "There is something I should like to do. And show you. Just the two of us. Will you come with me?"

"A Christmas morning errand with my wife?" He grinned at her. "Of course, I will." He kissed her cheek as if to emphasize the point, then continued up the stairs with her, the matter apparently settled.

## A Carol for Mrs. Dickens

The night passed for Kate with a series of dreams mingled with memories, both those she had visited and others she had not. Christmas was woven throughout all of them, and there was a delightful medley of songs from her youth and adulthood accompanying the visions. But ultimately, Kate woke early, eagerly waiting for the moment when enough would be enough and she could rise and start her day.

At long last, the light began to peek through the partition in the curtains, and she rose, the excitement within her creating sparks throughout her body, just like it had when she was a child. It was all she could do to contain her squeals and eager giggles as she changed from her nightgown into an ensemble for the day. She was in the process of pinning up her plait in a simple chignon when Charles stirred in their bed.

"Kate?" he mumbled, pushing up.

She turned in her chair, grinning. "Good morning. Merry Christmas."

He smiled sleepily, a faint light entering his expression. "Merry Christmas. Is it time to do your Christmas errand?"

REBECCA CONNOLLY

"It is," she confirmed, reaching back to add another pin. "If you can rouse yourself, we'll be back before the children come down."

"Consider me roused." Charles clambered out of bed and began dressing himself for the day.

Kate returned to her hair and threaded a ribbon into the arrangement as well. It was Christmas, after all. Then, almost as an afterthought, she picked up the sprig of holly she had worn before, not entirely certain what she would do with it but loving the Christmas talisman and wanting it close all the same.

Once they were prepared, Kate led them both down to the kitchens, where Mrs. Rook was already working to assemble the breakfasts.

"Oh, Mrs. Dickens! And Mr. Dickens. Merry Christmas to you." She bobbed a quick curtsey, smiling broadly.

"Merry Christmas, Mrs. Rook!" Charles boomed in his jolly way, making both women laugh.

"We are just going to prepare a basket to take somewhere," Kate told Mrs. Rook. "But I would like you to

## A Carol for Mrs. Dickens

pass my thanks and good wishes to Mrs. Morley. She was so kind to me last night, and it was so appreciated."

The cook's brow furrowed, creating more lines than normal upon her face. "Mrs. Morley? I don't recollect a Mrs. Morley being here last night."

Kate smiled rather fondly at the memory of the woman. "You'll remember her. About my height, a little gray in the hair, rosy cheeks, ready smile, wore a sprig of holly on her apron and her cap."

Mrs. Rook shook her head, eyes widening. "No, I don't recall anyone like that being in the kitchens. Of course, I was running a bit ragged, so Lord only knows what names and faces fell out of my memory before it was all over."

A faint buzzing began in Kate's chest, the inclination rising to either laugh or awkwardly clear her throat. "I am sure that is it," she managed, still smiling in a confused sort of wonder.

"I'll just see to the breakfasts," Mrs. Rook said, scratching at her ear. "Then you'll have something hot when you return from your errand." She bobbed again and moved to another part of the kitchens.

*145*

How could Mrs. Rook not recollect Mrs. Morley? She had left an indelible impression upon Kate and surely with every other person she came in contact with. And she had known her way around the kitchen with such skill, she surely would have been an asset to Mrs. Rook.

"How big of a basket do we need?" Charles asked as he wandered over to a collection of them in a corner. "Big? Small?"

Shaking her head, Kate pointed toward one on the end. "That one there will do. An in-between size, I suppose."

She moved to the counter and began pulling some of the leftover food from the night before toward her. There was so much available and so much more being prepared for the day ahead that there was no shortage of options to be included. She had brought some woolen stockings and a warm shawl from upstairs, and she tucked them into the basket. There were some preserves jarred up nearby, so a few of the jars went into the growing pile as well.

She cast her eyes about the kitchens, wanting

A CAROL FOR MRS. DICKENS

something more to add, when her eyes fell on a nearby flour-speckled section of counter. Sitting almost exactly in the center of the white dusting was a sprig of holly, nearly glistening in the morning light, its deep-green leaves and rich-red berries practically a beacon of Christmas itself.

Kate looked at the holly she held in her hand—the one she had worn the night before—then at the holly on the counter. Where had that come from?

*A bit of Christmas magic*, her heart whispered.

Why not?

Kate grinned at the lone holly on the counter, every piece of the puzzle from the night before falling neatly into place in her mind. She pulled the ribbon from her hair and fastened her holly sprig to the basket, nodding in satisfaction when she finished.

This was a gift she would be delighted to give.

She plucked up the basket and gestured for Charles to follow as they left the kitchens and moved upstairs.

"Where are we going, Kate?" Charles asked as they bundled up in scarves and cloaks.

Kate smiled at him. "You'll see." She tied the

ribbons of her bonnet tightly, and they stepped out of the house.

The dawn seemed particularly bright this Christmas morning, the sun reflecting off the bits of snow along the paths and buildings. The windows had a sheen of frosted ice that reflected the sunlight in almost blinding fashion, adding to the glowing luster of the day. There weren't many people out and about this early, as was to be expected on such a day, but those who were out offered cheerful greetings of the season.

Charles and Kate returned those festive greetings with all their hearts, and Kate felt perfectly natural and easy walking arm in arm along the London streets with her husband.

And London, nor any other place in the world, had ever seemed so bright nor so beautiful. This Christmas morning, the whole world seemed perfectly designed to praise the Lord and rejoice in celebration of such a day.

The greenery adoring the streets was rich and deep in color. The red ribbons were brilliantly bright. The sun glowed with unmatched radiance in the clear, blue sky, and the light glinted majestically off every surface, be it

# A Carol for Mrs. Dickens

reflective or otherwise. Every face she saw was beaming with joy and merriment, and she could feel every ounce of that joy within her very soul. The echoes of the choir she had heard the night before returned, this time with great fanfare and a rousing accompaniment that begged to be sung aloud, yet the morning was still young, and no carolers had dared venture forth yet.

It was no matter. The song in her heart and mind would be more than enough until the rest of the city roused itself.

Kate could hardly contain her steps and her feelings in spite of the hour and relative quiet. Indeed, she felt as though some restless creature of warmth and delight could not be contained within her. She was not sure if she wished to cry or laugh or leap for joy, but any or all of those things might release this sensation. She might skip alongside her husband or join the imagined carolers in their singing or twirl about while tossing the small quantities of snow about her head and giggling like a schoolgirl. It was magical, this Christmas Day. Glorious, wonderful, and so very, very merry.

Kate had not felt merry in ages.

It was a refreshing sensation.

Charles whistled "The Holly and the Ivy" as they walked the few blocks that Kate had traversed the night before. He seemed content to simply be alive on this Christmas Day, and Kate was proud of it—and him. Her husband with his distraction, contentment, enthusiasm, and passion. His drive and his ambition, but most of all, his view of the world and his determination to improve upon everything he saw. His impossibility to ignore those in need and his complete belief that humankind could be better than they were.

He asked no questions as to their destination or Kate's reasoning, for which she was grateful. She had no notion how to explain what had happened to her or how changed she felt this morning. She wasn't even certain she could tell him why she had noticed those children on the street corner yesterday, let alone gone for a walk and followed them home during the night.

But she had known what she would do, if at all possible, and that was what she was doing.

If it was possible to give someone a merrier Christmas than the one they were experiencing, should she

## A Carol for Mrs. Dickens

not do all within her power to see it done? After the gift she had been given the night before, after being nurtured, revived, and renewed with the Christmas Spirit by her very own memories, she now had the power to share that very same spirit and magic with someone else. To give such a gift that someone else might also be lifted as she had been.

They reached the street filled with the poorer houses where she had heard such singing the night before. All was quiet now, a hushed, reverent sort of peacefulness.

Kate glanced at Charles and saw his eyes darting from house to house and from broken window to tattered curtains. A somberness filled his features, but there was no judgment in his expression, no disgust or disgruntlement to be found in his eyes or the turn of his mouth. He simply saw, with his own eyes, the status of these creatures, his fellow man, and in seeing, could begin to understand.

Kate's heart warmed. Would that all men could be more like him in that regard. Would that her children could be too. Would that she might always see, as her father had done, God's children as such.

Kate led Charles down the row of houses until they reached the one with crates before the door.

She knocked gently but firmly, then stepped back, directly beside Charles. She glanced down at her hands, noting her soft gloves and recollecting the hands of the poor, weary mother she had seen the night before. With quick, jerky motions, she tugged off her gloves and tucked them into the side of the basket, blinking back tears as the image of her father and his scarf rose into her mind.

This was what Christmas was about, what the Lord was about, and what Kate hoped to be about as well.

The door creaked open, and the father she had seen the night before appeared, looking startled that anyone should be calling upon him.

"Yes?" he asked hesitantly, taking in their appearance.

Kate smiled indulgently. "Merry Christmas, sir. To and to your family. My name is Catherine, and this is my husband, Charles."

Charles tipped his hat, smiling as well.

The man nodded in acknowledgment. "Merry Christmas to you, ma'am. Sir. How can I help you?"

"You may help us," Kate told him with a slight heft to the basket she held, "by taking this basket for your family."

He started to take it, then looked at her in surprise. "For my family?"

"Indeed, sir." Kate was beaming now and practically shoved the basket into his hands. "For your family this beautiful Christmas morning. Please, do take it."

"Please," Charles insisted without hesitation.

The man did so, looking at the contents in astonishment, then back at them with a smile and soft eyes. "Thank you so much. This is most generous of 'ee."

"It is Christmas," Kate reminded him. "We ought to do good and be good, and I have seen your little ones out selling sprigs of holly. If they can bring light and joy and festivity to the neighborhood, then so can I."

"It is hardly a comparison," he protested, looking behind him.

Kate shook her head. "I disagree, if you'll allow

me. We all do what is in our power. Sometimes that is more temporal, and other times it is more symbolic. But it is all good, and it is all from the heart."

She felt Charles's arm slide around her waist, pulling her closer to his side. She had never felt his love nor his approval more strongly, and her heart could have burst into delightful flame.

The children appeared at the door, looking into the basket eagerly.

"Good morning, children," Kate greeted happily. "Merry Christmas!"

"Merry Christmas!" came their cheerful replies.

The little boy looked at her and Charles with a bright smile. "Would you like to come in? Papa has finished carving the Nativity, and he's about to tell it."

"Oh, Joe, I don't think that they—"

"We would love to listen to the Nativity story," Charles overrode in a rough voice. "If your father consents."

Looking even more bewildered, the father stepped back. "O-of course, sir. Ma'am. 'Tis only a simple carving, and everyone knows the story—"

## A Carol for Mrs. Dickens

Charles put his hand on the man's arm as though they were old friends. "It is the most important story, and this is the day of all days to hear it. Please, do tell it."

Understanding passed between them, and Kate stepped forward to take the hands of the pregnant wife and mother, who was already teary. The children ran about the small space in excitement, either for the story or for the basket but entirely for Christmas.

On the floor before the fire were a dozen rough figures hewn out of wood. Kate could make out four sheep, a cow, a donkey, three men, an angel, and a kneeling woman, all encircling the babe in a manger she had seen him carving the night before. As the father closed the door to the house, the children sat on the floor, facing the figures.

"A very long time ago," he began as he sat on the floor beside the carvings, picking a few up, "in a place called Bethlehem, a man named Joseph brought his wife, Mary, to pay their taxes. But Mary was carrying a baby within her, and it was going to come any day. When they got to Bethlehem, there were no rooms in the inns or homes there. No place to rest, and no place for the baby to be born."

The little girl clapped her hands over her cheeks, concern etched on her sweet face.

"Mary and Joseph found a stable," the father went on, "which is like a barn. And there the baby Jesus was born. An angel came and told shepherds in the fields nearby that the Savior had been born and that they should go and see." He lifted the angel to show the children, then set him back down. "So they came to the stable as fast as they could." He indicated the

## A Carol for Mrs. Dickens

shepherd figures and their sheep. "And they wor-
shipped the baby Jesus, then went and told everyone
they could. And they heard in the heavens many, many
angels, who all said, 'Glory to God in the highest, and
on earth peace, good will toward men.'"

The children gaped at their father with open
mouths, then down at the figures themselves.

"Good will toward men," Kate murmured for herself alone, shaking her head in wonder as her hand
smoothed her rounded belly.

"Aye, ma'am, as 'ee have shown," the mother replied with equal softness, her pose much the same.

They shared a knowing smile, and Kate reached a
hand toward her again, squeezing it fondly when she
took it.

"And Jesus is everything, aye?" their father asked
the children.

They both nodded rapidly.

"And He did good things His entire life," he continued. "He still does good things in our lives. So we
do good things in our lives to be like Him and to
thank Him for everything. Today is Christmas, so we

celebrate the blessings in our lives. We may not have much, but we have each other, and we have joy. We have Jesus. And soon we'll have a new baby too."

The children looked at their mother, who rubbed her swollen stomach on cue, smiling through her tears.

Kate felt her own child dance within her as though inhabiting Charles's enthusiasm for Christmas already, and she could not help but to pat it lovingly in response.

"And we have our new friends," the little boy shouted, looking at Kate and Charles. "Who bring us nice things at Christmas!"

That made them all laugh.

"Yes, we do," his father replied, meeting Kate's eyes with real gratitude. "God has truly blessed us, hasn't He?"

His children agreed and began to play with the nativity figures.

"Thank you for this," their mother said to Kate in a soft voice. "I don't know what we did to deserve your kindness, but . . ." She trailed off, shaking her head in disbelief.

## A CAROL FOR MRS. DICKENS

Kate could only smile at her. "You didn't need to deserve it, my dear. It is Christmas. The season of giving and goodwill. It is my pleasure to give these gifts. And I should like to do more, if I may."

"Mrs. Dickens—" the woman began.

"You know who we are?" Charles interrupted with a laugh.

She grinned almost sheepishly. "I saw a speech you gave at a charity last month, sir. It was quite memorable. Very good of you."

"We do what we can," Charles replied, rubbing Kate's back. "But the beauty of this Christmas morning is all due to my wife. She is the angel of our home and the conscience of our family."

Kate nudged Charles half-heartedly, her cheeks warming with a blush. "I just wanted to help. And I love Christmas."

"Who doesn't?" her new friend agreed, looking at her husband and children on the floor.

Kate shook her head at the irony. She had not loved Christmas this year in the least, and even the day before she had not been convinced it would be a holiday worth celebrating. But after a series of personal memories and miracles, she had found herself here, in this small, poor house with a family in need, and felt a true love of the holiday, of the season, and of everything surrounding it.

She did love Christmas. That was as miraculous as anything else, among all that had happened and the wisdom and insight she had gleaned.

All was not perfect, but all would be well. And that was enough.

She had found Christmas, alive and well within her life and her memories, and now in her heart as well.

On that beautiful, bright Christmas morn, Kate Dickens could truly agree that she had also been blessed in so many ways. Beyond expectation, beyond reason, beyond deserving, beyond imagination.

Truly, deeply, undeniably blessed.

Swallowing a lump in her throat, Kate could only think of one thing to say that would befit the moment. "God bless us every one."

Charles took her hand, squeezing hard and blinking rapidly as his tears fell, repeating, "Every one."

# $\mathscr{A}$CKNOWLEDGMENTS

Thanks to Lisa Mangum for geeking out about this with me from day one, and to Heidi Gordon and Callie Hansen for joining us from day two. Thanks to Heather Moore and Hannah Groesbeck for early reading and notes. And thanks to Simon Callow for his dedication to the life of Dickens, which made my workload so much more convenient.

# ℬIBLIOGRAPHY

Callow, Simon. *Dickens' Christmas: A Victorian Celebration*. Harry N. Abrams, Inc., 2003.

"Christmas Puddings—from Mrs Beeton to Elizabeth David." https://library.leeds.ac.uk/special-collections/view/816. 2024.

Dickens, Charles. *A Christmas Dinner by Charles Dickens*. Red Rock Press, 2014.

Elsna, Hebe. *Unwanted Wife: A Defense of Mrs. Charles Dickens*. Jarrolds, 1963.

Halliley, Mark, and Sue Perkins. "Mrs. Dickens's Family Christmas." *BBC Two*. https://www.youtube.com/watch?v=yYjhOi62Bj8. 2011

Kelly, Helena. *The Life and Lies of Charles Dickens*. Simon and Schuster, 2023.

Nayder, Lillian. *The Other Dickens*. Cornell University Press, 2012.

## BIBLIOGRAPHY

Rossi-Wilcox, Susan M. *Dinner for Dickens*. Prospect Books, 2005.

"Sketches by Boz, by Charles Dickens." https://www.guten berg.org/files/882/882-h/882-h.htm. Updated April 20, 2021.

Standiford, Les. *The Man Who Invented Christmas: How Charles Dickens's* A Christmas Carol *Rescued His Career and Revived Our Holiday Spirits*. Broadway Books, 2017.

# Victorian Christmas Traditions and History

## Christmas Trees

This most festive of Victorian Christmas traditions can be traced back to Queen Victoria's marriage to Prince Albert, who was born in Germany, where decorated trees were a tradition of the season. In 1848, a drawing of the Royal Family celebrating around a decorated tree was published, and it wasn't long before homes all around Britain were sporting resplendent trees with candles and homemade decorations at Christmastime. While Queen Charlotte, wife of King George III, was the first monarch with a Christmas tree in England, it was Prince Albert who made it popular.

## Christmas Cards

Children were encouraged to write messages to their family during the season, but it wasn't until the arrival of

VICTORIAN CHRISTMAS TRADITIONS AND HISTORY

the Penny Post in 1840 and the dawn of the Industrial
Age that Christmas cards became a de facto part of celebrating the season. In 1843, civil servant Henry Cole
was the first to commission an artist to design a card
for sale. These first cards were too expensive for everyone, but the idea caught on, and children began making
their own. As technology advanced and printing became
cheaper, the price dropped, and alongside the introduc-
tion of the halfpenny postage rate in 1870, the Christmas card industry quickly took off.

## Christmas Decorations

Homes had been decorated with evergreens since
medieval times, but the tradition became much more
elaborate thanks to the Victorians, who included
wreaths, ivy ribbons, tree ornaments, and mistletoe balls.
Families put up decorations and greenery throughout the
house on Christmas Eve. Boughs, garlands, and sprigs
decorated windows, tables, mantels, and stairways with
the scents and colors of the season. For those who could
not go out and cut their own, greenery could be purchased. The greenery remained in place until Twelfth
Night when it was removed and burned lest it bring bad

luck to the house. By the 1880s, decorations were being mass-produced for all to enjoy.

## *Christmas Gifts*

Gift giving traditionally occurred at the new year, but it moved as Christmas became more important to the Victorians. At first, gifts remained as modest as ever—fruit, nuts, sweets, and small, handmade trinkets—and hung on the Christmas tree. However, as giving presents took center stage and the gifts became bigger, they were placed under the tree. Though gift giving did not occupy the forefront of the Christmastide season, people did give gifts, including on St. Nicholas Day, Christmas Day, and Twelfth Night.

## *Christmas Turkey*

A midwinter feasting festival stretches back for centuries, but the festive turkey first appears in England in the sixteenth century, with Henry VIII purportedly being the first monarch to dine on it at Christmas. The tradition of a feast rapidly spread throughout the country, but it was still prominently goose on the Christmas table until the Victorian era. A famous Christmas dinner

VICTORIAN CHRISTMAS TRADITIONS AND HISTORY

scene appears in *A Christmas Carol*, where Scrooge sends Bob Cratchit a large turkey.

## *Christmas Entertainment*

Holiday entertaining, the central feature of Christmastide celebrations, began around St. Nicholas Day and extended to Twelfth Night. Small social gatherings, dinner parties, house parties, masquerades, balls, and home theatricals filled the intervening weeks.

The holidays were a time of games as well, and the game of Snapdragon was a popular one. It was played by placing raisins in a broad, shallow bowl, pouring brandy over them, and then setting the brandy on fire. Players showed their courage by reaching through the spirit-flames to snatch up the raisins. The game even came with its own song:

> *Here comes the flaming bowl,*
> *Don't he mean to take his toll,*
> *Snip! Snap! Dragon!*
> *Take care you don't take too much,*
> *Be not greedy in your clutch,*
> *Snip! Snap! Dragon!*

# A Christmastide Calendar

Some of the traditions and dates that might have been observed during Victorian-era Christmas celebrations included:

**Stir It Up Sunday**

On the fifth Sunday before Christmas, the family would gather to "stir up" Christmas puddings that needed to age before being served at Christmas dinner.

**December 6: St. Nicholas Day**

In a tradition from Northern Europe, this day might be celebrated with the exchange of small gifts, particularly for children. House parties and other Christmastide visiting also began on or near this day.

**December 21: St. Thomas Day**

Elderly women and widows went "thomasing" at the houses of their more fortunate neighbors, hoping for gifts of food or money. Oftentimes, landowners cooked

## A Christmastide Calendar

and distributed wheat, an especially expensive commodity, to the "mumpers" who came begging.

### December 24: Christmas Eve

Holiday decorating happened on Christmas Eve when families cut or bought evergreen boughs to deck the house. The greenery remained in place until Epiphany when it was removed and burned lest it bring bad luck.

### December 25: Christmas Day

Families typically began the day with a trip to church, often picking up a Christmas goose from the local butcher on the way home. Though gifts were not usually exchanged on Christmas, children might receive small tokens, and cottagers might give generous landowners symbolic gifts in appreciation for their kindness. The day culminated in a much-anticipated feast. Traditional foods included boar's head, brawn, roast goose, mincemeat pies, and the Christmas puddings made a month earlier.

### December 26: St. Stephen's Day or Boxing Day

After receiving their Christmas boxes, servants usually enjoyed a rare day off. Churches distributed the money from their alms boxes.

Families might attend the opening day of pantomimes. The wealthy traditionally enjoyed fox hunting on this day.

## A Christmastide Calendar

**December 31: New Year's Eve**

Families thoroughly cleaned the house before gathering in a circle before midnight to usher out the old year and welcome in the new.

Some Scots and folks of Northern England believed in "first footing"—the first visitor to set foot across the threshold after midnight on New Year's Eve affected the family's fortunes. The "first footer" entered through the front door and left through the back door, taking all the old year's troubles and sorrows with him.

**January 1: New Year's Day**

The events of New Year's Day predicted the fortunes for the coming year, with a variety of traditions said to discern the future, like "creaming the well" or the burning of a hawthorn bush.

**January 6: Twelfth Night**

A feast day honoring the coming of the Magi, Epiphany—or Twelfth Night—marked the traditional climax of the holiday season and the time when celebrants exchanged gifts. Revels, masks, and balls were the order of the day. With rowdy games and large quantities of highly alcoholic punch, they became so raucous that Queen Victoria outlawed Twelfth Night parties by the 1870s.